Jennison let loose with the scattergun as the four friends moved into a skirmish line

They dived for cover, giving Gooseneck and Reena time to scuttle from the back of the rig, the woman limping heavily as she ran for safety.

Ryan had flattened himself behind a live oak, squinting to one side of the gnarled trunk, seeing, to his horror, that Knuckles remained standing in the open.

"Get down!" he yelled, waving the muzzle of the SIG-Sauer to catch the youth's attention.

Reena saw him and fired a burst, the lead ripping through the snow-covered branches just above Ryan's head.

The one-eyed man's shout had no effect. The hunchbacked lad had turned away and was hopping toward the wag, where Reena and Gooseneck had taken cover.

When Knuckles was only a couple of stumbling steps away, the woman stood, her hair matted and tangled with the snow, and leveled the scattergun.

"No!" Ryan screamed.

Other titles in the Deathlands saga:

JAMES AXLER

DEATH LANDS®

Shockscape

A GOLD EAGLE BOOK FROM
WORLDWIDE®

TORONTO • NEW YORK • LONDON
AMSTERDAM • PARIS • SYDNEY • HAMBURG
STOCKHOLM • ATHENS • TOKYO • MILAN
MADRID • WARSAW • BUDAPEST • AUCKLAND

This is for Ian McKean and everyone at F. C. Greens who've worked to keep four wheels on my wagon for so many years. With my thanks.

Second edition April 1999

ISBN 0-373-62556-1

SHOCKSCAPE

Living close to the edge makes you feel a new man. And the new man wants to live even closer to the edge.

—from *Fresh Fields,*
    by Marcus Strafford

Chapter One

Ryan Cawdor blinked open his good eye and saw that the armaglass walls of the mat-trans chamber were a rich cobalt blue.

He drew a long, cautious breath. The instant, uncontrollable jumps the companions made from place to place generally left them feeling like their heads had exploded, then been reassembled by a team of blind triple-stupe muties.

"Not too bad," Ryan whispered.

No time seemed to have elapsed since he'd closed the door on an almost identical chamber in what had once been the thriving and bustling metropolis of Chicago. Yet Ryan knew that he and his friends would find themselves thousands of miles from their starting point.

Apart from a faint nausea, the one-eyed man felt fine. Sometimes a jump was accompanied by horrific hallucinations, like a combination of daydreams and nightmares. Images of death would flood through the mind, like eternal chases along

endless dusty corridors by faceless, gibbering spec-
ters.

This time Ryan could only vaguely remember
sunshine and fresh grass on a summer hillside, a
crystal stream over smooth boulders streaked with
a tracery of silver quartz, and Krysty Wroth at his
side, lying on her back in a thin cotton shift, green
eyes shaded by her arm, smiling.

Now, in the real world, Krysty was alongside
him, opening her emerald eyes, smiling up at him,
her hand lifting to brush back an errant strand of
her fiery crimson hair.

"Good jump, lover," she murmured.

"Known worse."

"Haven't known many better." The voice came
from the slightly built man, sitting cross-legged on
the floor, his back against the opposite wall. He
reached into a pocket of his coat and pulled out a
pair of wire-rimmed glasses, polishing them for a
moment on his sleeve before putting them on.

"True enough, J.B.," Ryan agreed.

The black woman who sat next to J. B. Dix was
also recovering. Mildred Wyeth was a medical
doctor and a brilliant shot with a pistol. She'd been
born in 1964, then cryogenically preserved in the
year 2000 when minor surgery went wrong.

The nuclear holocaust that destroyed much of
the world, and most of the people, had left her

frozen, only to be revived generations later by Ryan and his friends. One of Mildred's biggest problems had been coming to terms with the fact that a hundred years had gone by while she existed through the dreamless sleep. And that everyone she had ever known was now dead.

She stood, steadying herself on the armaglass. "Best jump I've been through. Now, if they were all like that I wouldn't mind doing it more often. No different from a stroll in the park."

"I want a pee, Dad."

Ryan's eleven-year-old son, Dean, had awakened and was investigating something in his right nostril.

"That's disgusting," Krysty told him.

"Better out than in." He grinned at her.

"That boy will undoubtedly go far. And the farther the better."

The sting of the remark was taken away by the cackle of laughter from the grizzled old man squatting next to J.B.

"How you feeling, Doc?" Ryan's right hand eased toward the butt of his P-226 SIG-Sauer 9 mm automatic.

Doc Tanner's mind hadn't been stable since a time-trawling experiment, focused on November 1896, had plucked him from his home, wife and children, and eventually, brought him forward to the Deathlands present.

It had been only an hour earlier that he'd been trying to return to his own time, so deranged that he'd fired a shot at Ryan from the massive Le Mat he wore on his hip.

Amazingly he now looked and sounded as near normal as he ever had.

The only one of the group of seven companions not yet recovered from the jump was their most recent addition, a youth once known as Brother Michael, from the isolated and enclosed religious order at Nil-Vanity, above Visalia in the California Rockies. Only nineteen years old, he shared with Doc the unique experience of having been successfully brought forward through time. In his case, from shortly before the United States of America ended and Deathlands began.

Being jolted to the new wastes had been difficult for the teenager to handle. But he'd made the adjustments, insisting on changing his name, reversing it to plain Michael Brother.

Now he was stirring, his dirt-caked bare feet shuffling on the floor. His long robe was rumpled, showing muscular thighs. The cord around his waist had worked loose, and two slim-bladed daggers clattered on the steel disk beneath him.

"I thought I was asleep back in the community," he said, brown eyes blinking.

"How do you feel, Michael?" Ryan asked.

"Not bad."

"That was a good jump, wasn't it, Dad? Can we get moving?" Dean rubbed his hands together. "Hey, it's cold."

Ryan stood, flexing the stiffness from his back. The boy was right. It did feel colder than usual.

Now everyone was standing, adjusting clothing and weaponry.

Krysty breathed in, long and slow, closing her eyes for a moment.

"Feel anything?" Ryan asked.

"No. Doesn't feel like anyone close. Usual redoubt kind of...dead and empty, and a sense of a long time gone."

Ryan drew the SIG-Sauer, hardly even aware of the familiar weight and balance, an extension of his own right arm. "Everyone ready?"

"Have we completed a jump, or are we about to commence one? If you will all forgive an old man's question."

Ryan glanced at Doc, seeing the confusion in the milky-blue eyes.

"Just made one, Doc. Got us away from Chi-town, remember?"

"Just got in from the Windy City and... How does it go on?"

Ryan caught the look of concern on Mildred's face. Doc's mind came and went. Sometimes it was close to normal.

Sometimes it wasn't.

Right now it looked as though the appalling experiences of the previous few days had either opened up some of the old scars or carved fresh ones.

"Doc, just stay close to me," said J.B., holding his Smith & Wesson M-4000 12-gauge cradled against his right hip.

"Stay close, my dear John Barrymore? Does the darkness gather? I am reminded of lines written by a clever fellow I met back in...whenever it was? Rexford. Eben Rexford. Odd how I can recall things from two hundred years ago and scarcely have any remembrance of what I ate to break my fast this morning."

Ryan had paused, fingers on the cold metal of the gateway's door handle. Looking back at Doc, it crossed his mind, as it had dozens of times before, that it might be a whole lot easier to put a full-metal jacket through the old man's skull.

The Trader would have done it. He would have said that anything that made your life easier and safer should be done.

But life would surely be a lot duller without Doc Tanner.

"We gotta be away from here, Doc," Ryan said quietly. "Let's go."

"Remember me when I am far away, far off in a distant land where—" Doc stopped. "No, that was not what Eben wrote. He wrote a beautiful song about having silver hairs among the gold." His voice lifted into a surprisingly melodic tenor. "'Shine upon my brow today, life is fading fast away.'"

Dean nudged his father. "Blade's broke off the hilt for Doc, Dad."

"Temporary, son," Ryan replied, keeping his fingers crossed that it wasn't permanent.

As THE HEAVY DOOR swung open, a distinct wave of cold air rushed in.

"Usually keep them at a steady temperature," J.B. observed. "Looks like the central master comp may have malfunctioned."

"Doesn't that mean that the gateway might not be working properly?" Mildred asked. "We might not be able to jump out of here. Wherever 'here' is."

"Could be."

Ryan looked out, seeing the usual mat-trans

setup—a small anteroom, unfurnished, and another closed door beyond that. Normally that would open onto the main control area.

"Ready?" he asked.

Chapter Two

The control section, with its banks of desks and flickering information processors was totally, clinically bare. The small room immediately next to the gateway was stripped. Normally there was some evidence of human habitation, even if it was only a single line of graffiti or a crumpled paper cup.

This time there was nothing—no table, no chair, no shelves on the off-white walls.

"Looks like we won't be finding too much in the way of food or supplies," Ryan commented.

Michael Brother was wandering around, stopping a moment to rub a finger along the tops of the brightly lighted consoles. "No dust."

"Air-conditioning keeps the delicate areas of the redoubt clean." Krysty looked around. "Whoever had the job of sealing up this place did it real well."

"Mothballing," Mildred said.

"What?" J.B. grinned at her. "That one of your twentieth-century sayings?"

"Yeah. Means sealing up against the elements. What they've done here."

Dean rubbed his hands together. "I'm cold and I want to pee."

"Wait until we get outside this part. There might be some warm clothes in another section of the redoubt, son."

"We going to open the sec door?" J.B. stood by the green lever that controlled the huge slabs of impenetrable armasteel.

"Red alert," Ryan said quietly.

At Ryan's nod the Armorer threw his weight against the lever, helped by Mildred.

Gears and counterweights rattled, and compressed air hissed.

Very slowly, like a dinosaur roused from slumber, the sec door began to rise.

Dean dropped flat on his stomach to peer under the door, his Browning Hi-Power in his right fist. "Nothing," he reported, his voice squeaking up the scale with tension.

Ryan knelt, looking below the rising wall of gray steel, into the familiar blank expanse of corridor. It had a high, rounded roof, with overhead strip lights and occasional tiny sec cameras.

J.B. checked the movement by returning the green lever to the central position, waiting for the word from Ryan to continue.

"Looks all right. Bastard icy wind blowing out there." He glanced out again. "Take it all the way up."

The sec door stopped with a jarring thud, about eighteen inches from the top. Ryan glanced up, seeing that the bare rock above it was cracked and rippled.

"I'll go first," Ryan said. "J.B. brings up the rear. Rest of you pick your own places. And let's take care."

SINCE THEY'D FIRST discovered the highly secret matter transmitters hidden in buried military redoubts, the group of friends had made a number of successful jumps, finding themselves in a variety of unexpected places.

Some of the high-tech complexes had been partly destroyed, and most had been stripped in the last days before skydark. Many had been found during the long winters, but it was a constant surprise to Ryan Cawdor how many still remained.

Not many of them had been as bitterly cold as this one.

Now that they were outside the comparative shelter of the control room, the temperature had fallen well below freezing.

Ryan hesitated. The corridor bent in both directions, but the chilly wind seemed to be cutting in from his left.

"Wait here," he ordered. "Dean and Krysty, come with me. Slow and careful."

"Some of the lights are out ahead," Dean said. "You can see the shadows change."

Ryan had already noticed, aware also of grittiness under the soles of his combat boots. The passage continued to bend away to the left, without a single door or side corridor.

"Wind's getting stronger." Krysty was hugging herself, her sentient hair curling around the sides of her face. "Got to be part of the redoubt collapsed somewhere up ahead."

"Yeah. Could've been a quake. Or mebbe the nukes coming in."

"Can I go ahead, Dad?"

"No."

"Please?"

"Careful, Dean. You know what the word 'No' means, don't you?"

The boy recognized the note of rising anger in his father's voice and kept quiet.

Ryan glanced up, seeing that the ceiling was furrowed with long, deep cracks, some of them exposing the rusted steel supports. The floor of the passage was littered with chunks of fallen concrete.

"What are these holes, lover?" Krysty pointed

with the muzzle of her own blaster, a 5-shot Smith & Wesson 640.

Ryan narrowed his eye, peering where she'd indicated. The stone was pitted with dozens of small holes, most about the size of a child's index finger. He poked at one of the bigger crevices, finding it went in deeper than he could reach.

"Looks almost like some sort of bugs been burrowing in," he said.

"Can I pee, Dad?"

"Sure. Do it up the side, against the wall."

"Don't look, Krysty."

"All right, Dean." She smiled at Ryan, making sure that the boy didn't see her.

She and Ryan had both noticed that Dean was becoming more self-conscious about his body. The first hesitant tendrils of pubic hair were already blossoming at his groin as he began the cautious ascent toward manhood.

Ryan and Krysty walked a little farther along the winding passage, into the teeth of what was now a strong, cold wind.

"Getting less gloomy ahead," Krysty said. "Looks like natural daylight."

Ryan nodded. Several of the light strips in the roof had gone out, but most of the red-eyed sec cameras still swiveled to follow their progress.

A few steps more and they saw what had happened. A huge slice of the land above the redoubt had vanished, hacked off along a fault line by a massive earthquake. It had cut clean through the tunnel, allowing bright sun to lance through, throwing sharp-edged shadows across a floor that was dusted with snow and patches of glittering ice.

Through the hole it was possible to see the dazzling blue-purple of the sky and the white-tipped peaks of distant mountains.

"The Darks?" Ryan asked.

"Old Utah, Montana or Wyoming. Or Colorado or the Tetons." Krysty shook her head. "Have to wait for J.B. to work out where we are."

Behind them, just out of sight, Dean Cawdor began to scream.

Chapter Three

There was no conscious movement.

Krysty's reflexes were cobra fast, but she was leaden compared to Ryan. He spun around, powering back along the corridor toward his son.

The cries were endless, rising up the scale, high enough to shatter crystal. It seemed impossible for the boy to keep on screaming without pausing for breath.

Dean was on his knees, his pants around his ankles, skin pale under the fluorescent lights. He was huddled over, hands grabbing at his groin, cupping his genitals. His head was bowed, his curly black hair tumbling over his ghostly face.

For a frozen splinter of time Krysty couldn't make out what was wrong with the boy.

There didn't seem to be any blood.

Yes, but only a threadlike trickle, running down the inside of one taut thigh.

He hadn't been shot.

Or knifed.

Couldn't have been.

Dean was close to the pocked surface of the concrete wall, near one of the most deeply pitted sections of the passage, adjacent to the honeycombed holes that Ryan had examined.

The scream stopped, and the boy turned his agonized eyes toward his father.

"Please..." he said, voice ragged. "Dad, will... please..."

Krysty was at Ryan's shoulder, poised for action. Farther down the corridor, beyond the kneeling boy, came the sound of running feet as the others responded to the scream.

The strip lighting in the ceiling of the passage was oddly deceptive. Just for a moment, Ryan had the passing illusion that the wall at Dean's back was moving, like a bizarre curtain of stone lace.

"What?" he asked helplessly.

His son answered by lifting his hands from his body, showing him.

"Oh, Gaia!" Krysty breathed, heartsick at the hideous sight.

Ryan said nothing, dropping the blaster on the floor, drawing the long-bladed panga from his belt and moving toward Dean.

It was a worm.

Deathly leprous white, its slender body twined around the young boy's penis and scrotum.

Ryan couldn't even tell for sure whether there

was only one of the coiling serpents, but it looked only like a single scaled body, about fifteen inches long. Nor could he see precisely what horrific wounds it was inflicting on his son.

But the trickle of blood had become a steady stream of bright crimson, pooling on the floor between Dean's combat boots.

There was a temptation to snatch at the creature and rip it away, stamp it into pulp.

Ryan hesitated, aware that the other four had joined them, half hearing their exclamations of loathly horror.

The hilt of the panga was slick in his fingers, and he felt like throwing up.

Dean's agonized eyes bored into him, and the boy kept whispering hoarsely, over and over again. "Please, take it away, Dad."

Now Ryan was close enough to be certain there was only one of the albino worms, and he could make out where its questing little head was buried in the fold of flesh between Dean's balls and his thigh.

Ryan reached out for it.

"No."

Mildred's voice penetrated through his anger, checking the movement of his hand.

"What, then?" he growled.

"Slow and easy, Ryan. Sudden movement and

it could open up the artery. Or you might snap off
its head, locked into the flesh. Got to make it let
go of the boy.''

''How? Come on, how?''

''Grip it behind its head. Finger and thumb.
Slow and easy, Ryan. Then, start to pinch it. Not
too hard at first. Slow and easy.''

Ryan laid down the panga, wiping his hand on
the leg of his pants, managing a grin at his son.
''Soon have the little fucker off you, Dean. Just
keep steady a minute longer.''

''Sure, Dad.''

The boy was looking beyond his father, out
along the corridor. Beads of sweat trickled down
his cheeks. His whole body was quivering, like an
aspen in a hurricane.

A tiny part of Ryan's mind noticed that everything had happened so fast that the small pool of
Dean's urine was still steaming in the cold air.

He eased in closer, trying to avoid the lashing
coils of the lean ivory worm. The head seemed to
be burrowing into the lad's flesh, as though it were
eating its way inward.

Out of the corner of his eye he saw again the
strange phenomenon of the concrete wall shifting
like a white curtain.

But he was concentrating on the venomous little
head of the creature. Now he could see its vivid

red eyes and the clamping jaws with a double row of needled teeth. Blood flecked its skin as it chewed through the boy's flesh.

Ryan's fingers were trembling, but he knew he had to go for it. Hesitation at this stage could be very terminal.

The scales of the albino reptile were smooth and slightly cold.

"Got it."

"Clamp it real slow, Ryan." Mildred was kneeling by his side, her breath frosting in the chill of the cavernous passage.

His finger and thumb were squeezing.

The worm pulsed, the jaws opening wider, and the body thrashed with an incredible whiplike tenacity. Dean moaned softly.

"Nearly done." He squeezed tighter, feeling its body pulsing against the pressure.

"Soon as its head comes clear, pull it right away, Ryan."

"Then…"

"Throw it over your shoulder and I'll do the rest," J.B. said.

"No, the pleasure of that will be entirely mine." There was the light sound of the steel blade of Doc's sword stick sliding free from its silver-topped ebony sheath.

"Yes, you fucker!"

The teeth had relaxed their grip, revealing a hole the size of a Magnum round on Dean's inner thigh. It was welling with blood.

Ryan tweaked the worm out with a snap of the wrist, jerking it savagely, cracking its spine like a buggy whip.

He tossed it behind him, where he heard the grating noise of Doc's rapier piercing the twitching, thrashing corpse.

"It is dead," Michael said.

But Ryan was too busy holding his son in his arms, embracing him, trying to stop the eleven-year-old from shaking apart.

"I'm not cryin', Dad, honest."

"I know you're not."

"Let me look at that bite, Dean. I'll put a dressing on it for you."

"No, Mildred. It's all right."

Ryan gripped the boy by the shoulders and grinned into his face, wondering whether he resembled the rictus of a death's head that he felt like.

"Listen, the number of people with real medical skill in Deathlands can be counted on the fingers of one hand, and Mildred is one of them. So, be a man and let her look at the bite."

Slowly, reluctantly, Dean moved his hand from the seeping wound.

Mildred nodded. "Doesn't look too bad. I'll tear

up a bit of cloth and tie it around it. I think it's clean, Dean.''

He cleared his throat, nervously. ''Er, Mildred...''

''What is it?''

The boy beckoned her lower, whispering, so that only the black woman and his father could catch what he said.

''It didn't bite my...my cock, did it?''

''Look for yourself.''

''Didn't want to look. In case it had bitten me there and... You know.''

She smiled, careful not to laugh. ''Course I know. The thing nipped you on the top of the leg. Everything else around there looks in perfect shape, Dean.''

''Honest?''

''Honestly.''

''Pull your pants up for the time being,'' Ryan said. ''We'll get along the corridor, the other way, and see what we find. Mildred can dress your wound for you there.''

J.B. slung the scattergun. ''What's up ahead?''

''The North Pole by the damnable feel of that chill zephyr,'' Doc said, wiping the smeared remnants of the white worm off his sword blade before carefully inserting the steel once more into the silver-headed walking stick.

"The tunnel's been chopped in half by a quake," Ryan said.

"We were just looking out at it when we heard Dean having a little trouble."

Dean scowled at Krysty, buckling his belt. "Like to see how you'd have felt with the sort of fucking 'little trouble' attacking you!"

"I'd probably have fainted dead away," Michael stated. "It was vile."

"The Great Worm Ouroboros," Doc intoned. "A creature from the deepest bowels of wind-washed nightmare."

He leaned his hand against the wall at his side, striking a dramatic pose.

The cold stone erupted with the hideous bleached snakes, several of them crawling with unbelievable speed onto his arm.

Chapter Four

"By the Three Kennedys!" Doc mopped at his brow with his swallow's-eye kerchief.

The walls had seethed with the lean, vicious snakes. Ryan's odd vision of the pocked concrete appearing like a curtain of shimmering white lace had turned into a grim reality. There were dozens and dozens of the creatures, writhing from countless small holes in the stone.

J.B. was wiping reptilian blood from the toes of his combat boots. "Trader used to say that a man who knew when to run away would be able to run away on another day."

Fortunately none of them had been badly bitten by the albino mutie snakes.

Doc had leaped and yelled, managing to shake off his sinuous attackers before any of them could reach exposed skin.

Michael had gone to his aid and had suffered from wearing the loose robe, his bare feet and legs now streaked with fresh blood.

But Mildred, having treated Dean's nasty

wound, had cleaned the young man's bites, announcing that none of them was serious.

The only answer to an infestation of wriggling evil was to run.

Dean had led the way, with Mildred at his heels. Doc had come last, hobbling at his best pace, helped by Michael on one arm and Ryan on the other.

The walls of the corridor, in the other direction, past the entrance to the mat-trans unit, were unmarked by the burrows of the worms.

It was also a little warmer.

They had passed a number of smaller sec doors in their flight from the wriggling menace behind them, but all were locked.

"Wish I could pick up some more plas ex," J.B. said. "Always comes in useful."

They'd stopped for a few minutes' rest in the center of the corridor, about two hundred yards beyond the entrance to the gateway. There was a sharp, consistent curve to the tunnel, and Ryan was beginning to suspect that they might eventually come on the broken walls from the opposite direction.

Michael had begun to pad off on his own, but Ryan called him back.

"Not alone."

"Just wanted to look a bit ahead. I won't go too far."

"You won't go *anywhere*. Not if I say not to, Michael. Understand?"

There was a streak of anger in Ryan's voice that Michael recognized. It would have been a triple stupe who chose to ignore it.

Ryan saw the expression on the young man's face and he shook his head. "We walk together or we fall together, Michael. If any of us tries to walk alone, he risks his own life. But he also hazards the life of everyone else."

"Yes, sorry. It will take some time to get used to being away from Nil-Vanity. As an oblate there, life had its restrictions, but you didn't get shot or attacked by a million white snakes if you stepped wrong. Sorry about that."

RYAN'S SUPPOSITION about the tunnel being circular wasn't tested, because they eventually found a sec door that was open, giving them access to the rest of the redoubt.

Once inside the core of the military establishment, the seven companions were able to move freely from section to section. It didn't take them long to explore the entire base.

When they returned to the cramped living quarters, Ryan sat on one of the metal bed frames.

"Well, I reckon this has to be the smallest we've seen."

J.B. pushed his fedora back off his forehead. "Guess so. And they did a real good job on stripping it cleaner than a dead dog in a stickie's cook pot."

The redoubt had obviously been used mainly for radar and space surveillance with a limited personnel but very tight external security. It appeared to have been built into the flank of a mountain, with only a restricted number of ob ports giving views of the outside world.

Everything that could be carried had been removed. Only fitted furniture, such as some cupboards and the beds, bolted to the floor, had been left.

The exception had been the mat-trans unit, obviously intact in case it needed to be used in some undetermined future.

But for the United States the only future was to become Deathlands.

"Still plenty of day left," Krysty said, peering through one of the domed windows.

"No reason to stay here longer," Ryan agreed. "At least we can go outside and take a look around. Then J.B. can use his microsextant and give us an idea where we are."

The Armorer had once had access to one of the

best collections of old maps in the country, courtesy of the Trader. Now they traveled light, but J.B. had retained the main cross-references in his encyclopedic memory, enabling him to place their location with a fair degree of accuracy.

Doc joined Krysty. The land stretched out ahead of them, the snow on the peaks tinted a light violet color from the chem-tainted sky.

Ryan knew that in the old days, before the long winter, the heavens would often be a bright, unsullied blue from east to west. Now it was very rare that it wasn't marred by pink or purple, the inheritance from the nuking nearly a century ago.

"My belief is that we are not a thousand miles away from Colorado," Doc said. "The contours of the mountains around us lead me to this supposition." He paused. "Then again, it could be New Mexico." Another pause. "Or New Hampshire. New Haven. New lamps for old."

"COLORADO," J.B. announced. "Difficult to remember the precise coordinates, but I reckon we're a way west of the big ville of Denver. Could be a little to the south. Least we got a clear view of the sun to base it on."

They stood together outside the main entrance to the redoubt. It was extremely cold, but they were sheltered from the worst of the biting northerly wind by the bulk of the mountain that towered above them.

Ryan spotted immediately why this particular redoubt hadn't been found or entered.

They were on what would have probably been a visitors' parking lot, a flat area around a hundred feet across. The narrow blacktop that wound away from it had been severed a hundred yards down its descent toward the valley far below, most likely by the very same quake that had caused such devastating damage to the encircling internal corridor.

Millions of tons of rock had slid across the highway, clipping the edge of the redoubt and blocking any direct view of the complex from lower down the hillside.

The snow around them was almost virginal, marred only by the delicate prints of small deer or goats. Dean had spotted them with interest.

"Could go hunting, Dad," he said eagerly. "Need some food."

It was true enough.

"Odds are we'll find more game down in the valley. See the silver line of a river? In among the pines. We'll get down there, if we can. Should be able to hunt some meat." Ryan glanced across at J.B. "That the way you see it?"

"Reckon so. Could do with finding somewhere for the night. It's already around ten below. Get in the wind and you drop another ten or more. By the time we work our way down over this snow it'll be closing in on night. Then we're looking at thirty below. Need a fire and shelter.''

THE OUTER SEC DOOR, with the usual code of 352 to open it, reversed to close it, had been shut behind them.

Ryan stood still, scanning the vista of peaks and valleys that stretched around them. As far as his eye could see there was no sign of any human habitation. No smoke rising and not a building anywhere.

He'd been up around Colorado with the Trader on several occasions, and he knew that there were a number of powerful barons with fortified villes set in isolated parts of the region.

But that was the past.

Few people knew better than Ryan Cawdor how fragile and temporary was the grip of most barons. Not many lived out their allotted span and died peacefully in their beds.

"Wish you'd gotten some decent boots, Michael," Mildred said. "I may have medical skills, but I can't do much for you if you get frostbite in your bare feet." When he simply shook his head, the doctor gave a short, barking laugh. "Except cut your toes off real neat."

They started off toward the lower ground, leaving the redoubt behind them.

Chapter Five

It hadn't taken long to construct a rudimentary shelter from fallen branches, lacing them to give protection from the wind, though the surrounding forest cut out most of the chill factor.

Ryan had scouted around, seeing plenty of tracks along a trodden path that wavered along toward the water. The river itself was about sixty feet wide, iced at the edges, but still clear near the rapid flow at its center.

As well as the pecked spoor of deer, there were some other tracks.

He called J.B. to come to look at them, while the other carried on readying the camp for the night.

J.B. whistled between his teeth. "Dark night!"

"You reckon same as me?"

"Bear?"

The pad marks were truly enormous, better than two feet in width, earth pressed flat beneath the weight of the creature.

J.B. bent and laid his own hand in the track. "Grizzly, I guess."

"Mutie animal?"

The Armorer straightened. "Must be. Paws that big and it's got to be well over twelve feet high. Could be bigger."

Both men stared into the deep, dark woods around them, aware that the bear that had recently passed by could be a whole lot bigger than twelve feet high.

IT WAS COMMON KNOWLEDGE that most hunting animals would avoid man, certainly not come close to a campsite where there was a good fire blazing.

The biggest danger was if you had fresh-killed meat in your camp. Particularly if it was a succulent haunch of bloody venison. There were enough legends about hunters waking up to find a hungry bear or a big cougar inside their tent, helping itself to their next day's food. Sometimes helping itself to them while it was at it.

But when you got to thinking about a mutie grizzly big enough to leave that sort of track, and you realized that you were thinking about a ton of red-eyed killing madness, something that could certainly run much faster and swim much faster than any person, you posted a watch for the night.

The companions decided to take turns.

It was the long hours after midnight, with the heart slowing and the breathing gentling down, when the risks of attack were highest.

Dean had been allowed to take the first guard, being replaced by Doc. Mildred came third, with J.B. choosing to sit up with her, keeping the fire charged with wood. Michael was awakened by J.B. two hours later.

Ryan and Krysty had decided that they'd carry the last two hours of the night through to the dawning together.

Michael had been warned about how to wake someone up in the middle of the night without making a lot of noise. You didn't clamp your hand over their mouth and expect that to do the trick.

Clamp your hand over Ryan Cawdor's mouth while he was deeply asleep and you'd find your lungs dangling out of your ass.

Michael knelt a few inches from Ryan and Krysty and whispered to him.

"Something's coming," he hissed. "Something coming this way."

Ryan was instantly awake, his nerves racing, his fingers automatically going to the butt of his SIG-Sauer.

"What?" he whispered.

"Noise in the undergrowth."

Krysty was also awake, pulling on her dark blue

Western boots, with the silver chiseled toes and the silver spread-winged falcons on the sides.

"Human, mutie or animal?" she asked.

"Don't know."

Ryan was on his feet, head on one side, straining to listen.

The forest at night was full of sound—the wind sighing through the frosted branches of the pines, crystals of ice tinkling down onto the hard, frozen ground.

But he could hear what Michael had heard, as could Krysty.

"Men?" she mouthed.

Ryan shrugged. At night in the woods it was impossible to tell the difference. But whatever it was, was heading their way.

Chapter Six

"Yo, the camp!"

Ryan and Krysty had awakened the others, and all of them moved back from the bright light of the fire. They melted into the surrounding trees, able to see without being seen, able to use their own blasters without being shot at.

"Yo, the camp! Three hunters here. We want some of that good heat."

Ryan glanced at J.B. "Could be a trick," he said quietly.

"Used it often enough ourselves in the old days, when we rode with Trader," J.B. replied, grinning tightly.

You ordered in a couple of men or women from your killing party. They made a lot of noise and attracted the attention of the camp, while you sent the rest of your group around the other side to come in from the back and coldcock them.

It wouldn't work against wily sec men, but against the normal run of stupes it was generally a sure-chill winner.

"Hey there! Just the three of us. Hunters. Working here in the lands of Baron Alferd Nelson, owner of the ville of Vista."

J.B. moved a step closer to Ryan. "Can't hear anyone behind us."

"Nor me." Ryan raised his voice. "We hear you. Come toward the fire, where we can see you. Hands out and showing."

"You're a careful man."

"Got some careful men standing around with blasters."

"How about some of you showing yourselves first, mister?"

Ryan shook his head in the velvet shadows. "Wasting time."

"Not sociable, mister!"

"Never said I was. You and your two friends want to come in here and warm up by our fire, then you're welcome."

"But?"

"But it's our fire, and that makes it our terms. I don't mind much what you decide, but make it quick, will you?"

There was a pause, and they could hear muttered conversation. Ryan gestured with his own blaster to the others on either side, reminding them to keep ready and alert.

"Yo, the camp?"

"I heard you."

"Coming in, like you said."

"Hands showing?"

"Sure, mister, hands showing."

THREE MEN WALKED slowly into the ring of light, the white of their palms showing against their dark clothes.

"Hold it there," Ryan called when they were close to the center of the small clearing, facing the brushwood shelters.

"What now, mister? Shit, I never known such a suspicious bastard."

"The blasters. Put them down by your feet. And that haunch of venison you got across your shoulder. Lay that down."

"You going to steal our food, stranger?"

Ryan's temper, never that far below the surface, snapped.

"Fireblast! We could've chilled you the moment you appeared. Put the bastard guns down. And the meat. And then we can all stop fucking around like gaudy sluts with their tits caught in a mangle."

"Lover!" Krysty chided at his shoulder.

"Well, they got me seriously pissed," he explained in way of apology.

Three rifles and two handblasters went down in the dirt, followed by the great chunk of deer.

Ryan stepped forward, holding the automatic so that it covered the three hunters. "That's good," he said. "Real good."

THE LEADER OF THE TRIO was Andy Burne. He was in his late thirties and had a limp that he blamed on a wolverine he'd encountered in the old ruins of Leadville, not far away.

One of his companions was a man named Clint Kael. He was tall and silver-haired, with a craggy, suntanned face. When he spoke he revealed a mouth that was totally lacking teeth.

"Pulled 'em all meself when I had cabin fever up on the sky ridge yonder. Closed in for the winter. Drew a tooth a day for three weeks. Passed the time and kept me laughing."

Third was a short black man who spoke very little. His name was Al Vayre, and he wore a dozen knives slung about his chest and hips.

Andy offered them some of the slab of venison that they'd shot farther up the valley on the previous morning, which was fine with Ryan, who had been planning to take it anyway.

Once a slightly uneasy peace had been established, and the blasters had been handed back to the hunters, the conversation began to stutter along.

Clint asked the first important question. "Any

you folks seen a big grizzly, and I'm talking triple-shit big?''

"Saw tracks," Dean replied. "You after it?"

Al answered. "The baron could be real pleased to have it chilled.''

"Long as he doesn't find us hunting around his favorite mountains. This close to his fucking ville." Andy laughed.

"You mean you aren't really supposed to be here?" Krysty asked.

"Ace on the fucking line, lady," Clint said, cackling.

"Why?" Michael was sitting by the fire, warming his bare feet.

Burne stared at him. "You go around with no boots on in this weather and they'll be taking you off at the knees, sonny.''

Michael ignored him. "Why shouldn't you hunt here? Isn't this all the lord's country and all the creatures his?''

Doc's shoulders shook with merriment. "You're so young, dear child," he said. "And you will eventually come to see that nothing is free. Everything is spoken for by the powerful and wealthy. It was true in the 1890s, true in the 1990s, true now.''

"All power corrupts, Doc," Mildred said, tossing a broken branch into the fire. Behind her the sky was already beginning to lighten with the promise of the false dawn.

He nodded, picking a piece of gristle from between his excellent teeth. "I do find myself, just for this once, in agreement with you, madam. I once believed that I should dedicate myself to directing barbs against those who are corrupt. Then I discovered that those I had picked as my targets were only insignificant dwarfs, fiddling on the edges of power. True power and the true corruption lie buried, far deeper. I know that now."

That speech, coming directly from the heart, brought a temporary silence.

Then Al sniggered, hawked up phlegm and spit it into the fire. "Let Baron Nelson hear you talkin' that shit, old man, and you gonna get to be real cold meat, before you could get your dick out to take a last piss. Baron knows about power and he's the one that got it."

"Where's the ville? Vista, did you say it was called?" J.B. asked.

"Yeah. Seven miles or so down the stream," Andy replied.

"Might visit it," Ryan said. "Pay our respects, like."

"That your boy, mister? He's got your hair and color and way of looking."

"Yeah, that's my dad," Dean answered.

Burne hesitated. "If he was mine, I'd take a wide course around Vista."

"Why?" Ryan leaned forward. "Come on, man, why do you say that?"

"Just a friendly word." Kael grinned. "You can take it or you can leave it."

All three men exchanged knowing glances.

Andy looked across at Ryan. Seeing the tension in his face, he changed the subject. "Where do you all come from?"

"South."

"Hired guns?"

"We do what we do," Ryan said.

"Yeah, sure. We just hunt. All we do. And keep away from the baron's sec men."

Clint squinted at his colleagues. "If we had these outlanders helping hunt the big grizzly, we could mebbe take him quicker and safer. Share us all some funning."

Andy nodded, looking around at Ryan and the six companions.

"Yeah. Then there'd be..." He hesitated. "Twenty of us." He saw the expressions on their faces and reconsidered. "Well, five of us. No." He counted painfully around the circle on his fingers, checking twice. "There'd be a full two hands...ten of us!"

Krysty leaned close to Ryan, whispering, "If he

wanted to count to twenty-one, he'd have to take his pants off.''

THE TRUE DAWN had come and gone. The three strangers had dropped off to sleep, lying where they slumped over, by the remains of the fire.

Ryan and the others had packed up their possessions and weapons, moving silently.

There was a certain attraction in going on a hunt for such a monstrous adversary, but not when it involved crossing the path of what sounded like a particularly hostile baron.

So they'd decided to move on.

Chapter Seven

It was a heaven of morning. The sky was clear, and there was hardly a breath of wind. Just a faint breeze, easing in from the far north.

The snow glistened in the sunshine, so bright it hurt the eyes to stare at it for too long. The temperature was still well below freezing, but without the wind it felt much warmer than it had the previous day.

Ryan breathed in, savoring the freshness. He was still able to catch the faint smoky scent of their fire, though the campsite was a good quarter mile behind them.

They were surrounded by mountains, and they'd all noticed the problems of being at altitude. Doc, in particular, was having trouble with his breathing, wheezing chestily. Mildred had guessed that they were probably close to ten or twelve thousand feet above sea level, from the effects of the scarcity of oxygen.

The physical results weren't pleasant. Ryan was aware of the blood drumming in his ears, his heart laboring that bit harder. And when he took in a deep breath, it felt as if his lungs weren't quite doing their normal job.

Dean scampered at his side. "Dad?"

"Yeah?"

"Why did you tell those three guys that we'd go hunt the grizzly with them?"

Ryan looked down into the boy's eager face. "Think you'd have liked that?"

"Sure. It'd have been a real hot pipe, wouldn't it?"

"Mebbe."

"Why we creep away like this?"

"They'd been up all night. Figured they'd crash out like they did."

"Yeah, but Dad, I never saw a real big bear like this one."

J.B. was close enough to overhear the conversation. "Even something that big could be difficult to track. Region like this one, the grizzly could be holed up somewhere and come out at you when you didn't expect it."

"Might take a long while," Ryan added.

THE RIVER WIDENED as they moved along its ice-bound banks.

As the sun rose, it pulled the temperature up with it. Away from the deep shadows, some of the snow began to melt, dripping from the tips of the branches of the pines.

The going was tough, with the water flowing into a steep-sided gorge, cascading in bursts of white froth over glazed boulders, its noise swelling to a deafening roar.

There was almost a holiday feel to the expedition, with Doc capering nimbly through the powdery snow, packing handfuls of it into wintery grenades and hurling them at Dean from behind trees. The boy gave back better than he got, twice scoring direct hits on Doc's face, splattering him with snow.

The path twisted and turned, with visibility never more than forty or fifty paces. The river boomed at their side.

J.B. had been walking along with Mildred, their arms linked like an old-fashioned courting couple, but he drifted away from her to join Ryan and Krysty at the back of the group.

Michael had also skipped on ahead, relishing the snowball fight with Doc and Dean.

"Ryan?"

"What? You worrying about there being sec men of the baron around? Could be we'll walk smack into them unknowing, what with the noise of the river and all."

J.B. nodded. He and Ryan had ridden together

long enough and fought together often enough to have developed an almost uncannily prescient understanding about what the other was thinking.

"Could be. Haven't seen any human tracks at all, but..."

The sudden noise that interrupted him was extraordinary, rising way up over the sound of the water.

First came screams, high and piercing, then came a thunderous roar that seemed to make the trees tremble.

"Oh, Gaia!" Krysty gasped, her hands going to her eyes, as though she were in pain. "It comes."

Chapter Eight

Dean was in the lead, with Doc slithering and stumbling at his heels, mouth gaping open in shock. Michael brought up the rear, skirts flying, bare feet pounding through the snow that carpeted the trail.

The grizzly bear was less than fifty paces behind him, but didn't seem to be in much of a hurry, as though it were utterly confident in its own speed, power and invincibility.

It was, quite simply, the biggest animal that Ryan Cawdor had ever seen. The paw prints hadn't prepared him for the massive bulk of the creature.

As it lumbered around the bend of the path, heading directly toward them, the ground vibrated. Snow spurted all around it. Breath steamed from its rank muzzle, and gobbets of froth dangled from its jaws.

It was more than twenty feet from nose to tail, and stood six feet tall at the shoulder as it loped along on all fours. A great hump of muscle rippled between the shoulders, the fur dark and tipped with flecks of silver.

Ryan stared into the blood-tinted eyes of Nature incarnate.

"Chill the fucker," he shouted.

But nobody could yet manage a clear shot at the charging animal. Dean, Michael and Doc were directly in the line of fire.

"Dark night!" J.B. cursed, bracing himself to open up with the Uzi on full-auto. "Get out the way! Dodge it!"

Ryan had the bolt-action SSG-70 Steyr rifle ready, the walnut stock pressed hard into the angle of his shoulder. He looked through the laser image enhancer, linked to the Starlite night scope, waiting for the moment to open fire.

Mildred had drawn her target revolver, the Czech ZKR 551, which was chambered to take six rounds of Smith & Wesson .38s.

Krysty had her snub-nosed double-action Smith & Wesson 640, though its two-inch barrel meant that it wasn't the best of weapons to stop a charging giant grizzly.

Dean had heard the warning shout from the Armorer, and he sidestepped like a quarterback from olden times dodging a rushing defensive lineman, slipping nimbly between trees to the right of the track, out of the line of fire.

Michael was struggling, his toughened bare feet sliding in the rutted ice and snow. His head was down, arms pumping, oblivious to anything that anyone might be shouting to him.

Doc was never cut out to be one of life's great sprinters. His eyes protruded, breath rasping in his chest, the altitude making everything much more difficult and painful for him. His cracked knee boots weren't any better than Michael's bare feet, and he slithered sideways, nearly falling. The mutie bear was less than twenty feet behind him.

"Get out the way, Doc!" J.B. bellowed, his finger twitching on the trigger of the 20-round Uzi machine pistol.

But Doc had a different idea.

Spinning and clawing out his Le Mat revolver, thumbing back on the hammer and steadying it, he aimed the portable Civil War cannon at point-blank range at the grizzly.

Ryan waited for the thunderous boom of the 63-caliber scattergun round that the antique Le Mat carried. But all he heard was the dry click of a misfire.

"By the—" Doc began, sounding slightly surprised.

The grizzly didn't break stride, swatting the old man out of its way with a casual sideways flip of one of its front paws. It lifted Doc off his feet, sending him spinning into a snowbank ten yards off the track.

As far as Ryan could see, the old man might not have been badly injured. But there wasn't time to check him out.

The first shots came from Dean.

From his new position among the pines, the boy had a clear shot at the grizzly's retreating flanks. He took the chance to fire three rounds from his Browning.

But he was out of breath, off balance and shooting between the trunks of trees. None of the bullets found their target.

"Get out of the fucking way, Mike!" Mildred screamed, risking a shot past the head of the running teenager.

It clipped the left shoulder of the galloping bear, bringing a deafening bellow of white rage from its drooling jaws.

Instead of checking its stride, the monster surged forward, taking everyone by surprise. It thrust out its muzzle and snapped at the fleeing Michael, catching the back of his robe, ripping it from neck to thigh.

The young man yelped in terror, pulling himself free and diving sideways toward Dean.

The bear reared up on its hind legs, head brushing snow from the higher branches of the surrounding trees, sending a sparkling shroud over itself. Its front legs clawed at the air, while a length of ragged cloth hung from its snarling teeth. There was a clotted patch of fresh blood on the shoulder where Mildred had managed to wound it.

For a trapped nanosecond of frozen time, the sight was so overwhelmingly impressive that nobody made a move.

Ryan broke the moment of stasis by squeezing the trigger on the Steyr, working the action smoothly.

The powerful round struck the bear high in the chest. A second bullet hit it in almost the same spot, producing a small spray of bright crimson blood that stained the snow around its feet. The bear responded with a quiet, puzzled snarl.

The two shots from Ryan seemed to release everyone from their momentary paralysis. The forest echoed with a sudden, savage burst of gunfire.

The grizzly roared, flailing its paws, snapping branches thirty feet in the air. Blood streamed from three dozen wounds, most of which would have proved terminal for any other animal.

But it was still on its feet, tottering, head weaving from side to side. One of Ryan's shots had taken out its left eye, and it wiped irritably at the bloodied socket as though it were trying to dislodge an errant fly.

"What's it going to take?" Krysty whispered.

"A nuke missile," Ryan replied.

The rifle in his hands was warm, empty.

At last the agonized, furious bellowing was beginning to weaken.

There was a noise behind Ryan and he spun, dropping the Steyr in the snow and drawing the SIG-Sauer, fearing that it might be the mate of the dying grizzly.

But it was Andy Burne, Clint Kael and Al Vayre, all holding their patched-up rifles, staring in slack-jawed amazement at the tableau of scarlet death in front of them.

"Holy fuck!" the black man said, taking an involuntary step away from the bloodied behemoth.

"I never, never..." Andy began, but the shock sent the rest of his words limping off into the vast silence around them.

The grizzly had slumped back to all fours, trying to focus on the creatures that had done this to it, still not aware of the imminence of its own passing.

"Mildred," Ryan called, lifting his voice over the animal's dying cries.

"Sure," she said.

Her face was set like black marble, eyes narrowed, regarding the behemoth along the barrel of her Czech target blaster.

The gigantic head lifted and the right eye rolled toward the group. The grizzly made a stupendous effort to raise itself onto its hind legs, but the wounds and the loss of blood thwarted the attempt. It simply stood there, blood dripping off the long muzzle into the snow.

"Sorry," Mildred said as she pulled the trigger and slammed a .38 into the mutie bear's brain.

Its legs crumpled under it and it rolled sideways with an awesome, ponderous grace, voiding both bladder and bowels over the crimson mud.

"That's it," Clint whispered. "That's done the bastard. We done the bastard. We done good."

The voice behind them was as cold as a glacier's heart. "Don't be too sure about that, boys. Baron Nelson might not agree with you."

Ryan Cawdor had ridden long enough with the Trader to recognize a sec man when he heard one.

Chapter Nine

"Trader?"

"Yeah."

"You said he was called Trader? Just that? Didn't have a real name?"

"Just Trader. Sometimes he was known as The Trader. Most times it was just Trader."

The old woman stared into the flames of the small fire. "Trader," she said, running the word around her mouth as though it were a succulent morsel of tender turtle meat.

Outside her hut, the narrow stream that would eventually become the mighty Sippi River fought its way past tangles of rotting trees, on through the shrouding ice. It had been snowing for the past couple of days, since Abe had been dropped off by the small wag that had given him a lift from the western outskirts of Chicago. The driver had been part Sioux, carrying home-brewed liquor between the scattered villes that lay between the Kotas and the Lakes.

"Name's Sees All Ways, and she's mostly

Chippewa," he'd told Abe. "Wisest shaman in all these parts. I'm linked to her by marriage through my grandmother's Running Deer clan. You want to know about this Trader guy, then she's the one to ask. I'll tell you how to find her."

The gunner from War wag One had become totally preoccupied with his quest. When Trader had taken his final, mysterious walk into the trees, Abe had been the last one to see him.

Everyone, including Ryan Cawdor, Krysty Wroth and J. B. Dix, had known for certain-sure that the tough old man was near his ending. He'd been torn apart by some kind of clawing cancer in his guts for months, and death had become the silent shadow, always at his shoulder.

Then Abe, recovering from near-mortal wounds, had begun to hear the rumors, whispers, shadows around a camp fire.

After his opportune meeting with Ryan and the others, Abe had tried to set it all behind him, placing the thought in a bolted cupboard in a locked room in the west wing of his memory. But however hard he threw away the key, he always woke in the morning to find it on his memory's pillow—Trader's alive.

It wasn't something that a man could easily cope with. It made sleeping difficult and set the brain to wandering at dangerous moments.

So Abe had decided to enter on his own private odyssey and track down the source of the ceaseless rumors.

Track down Trader.

Alive or dead.

SEES ALL WAYS THREW a handful of dusty powder onto the glowing embers of her fire. It gave off a rich, choking scent that made Abe's head spin. Images flashed into his mind—sunshine on a heather-covered hillside above the rolling plains of bloody old Kansas; salmon leaping in the rainbow spray of a waterfall in the Cascades; the shadows of evening surging up from the faint green ribbon at the bottom of the Canyon.

"This Trader was wise in the ways of the people?" the old woman asked.

"Some said he had a touch of native blood in him," Abe replied. "Shoshone, Paiute, Apache, Micmac, Nez Percé." The names rolled unbidden off the skinny little man's tongue.

"Enough," she said, her voice like a whiplash across his brain, stopping the litany.

Sees All Ways was a tiny figure, hunched under a patterned blanket, only her bird-bright eyes visible beneath the hood. Abe could see she wore a beautiful antique ring of turquoise, bound with whorls of beaten silver.

"You heard tell that he might still be this side of the dark river?"

She nodded very slowly. "I have heard this. But Trader is only a man."

"Special kind of man," Abe protested.

"He breathes and eats like other men. He dies like other men."

"Yeah, we all do. I just want to know for my own peace of mind..."

She nodded again. "I understand this. Sees All Ways met the Trader many times. In the tongue of the people we called him... How do you say it?" She hesitated for a hundred beats of the heart. Abe was conscious of the rising wind beyond the walls of the little cabin. "The Man Who Walks without Friends."

"No. Trader had friends."

"Close ones?"

It was the gunner's turn to nod. "Course. I knew men would of given their lives for him. I would of done it."

Sees All Ways coughed, a harsh, barking sound. "Perhaps the change between my words and yours..."

"You mean it sort of means something a little different in your language?"

"Perhaps."

"Try, please."

"A man who chooses his own trail through a desert place and takes no guidance from others. Yet is followed by others."

There was a sound like the creaking of an unoiled gate that Abe realized was the old Indian woman laughing to herself.

"What's funny? That sounds a much more true description of Trader."

"But it takes over four hands of your words and only one hand in the tongue of the people. That is funny."

"So, you still haven't said. Please, I *need* to know. Is he living? And if he is, then where can I go to find him?"

She delved into a little deerskin pouch around her wattled throat and pulled out eight or nine small pieces of bone, polished with age to golden ivory. Sees All Ways dashed them to the dirt floor of her hut with surprising venom.

"There," she said, spittle flying into the fire, hissing on the hot stones. Abe leaned forward to peer at the jumbled pattern, unable to perceive any shape to it.

"What's it tell you?"

"It... I do not understand this."

"What? All you have to do is tell me if he's alive and point me toward him. Not asking you to come along with me."

"The bones tell me that Trader probably lives. Probably."

Abe punched his right fist into his left palm. "Ace on the fucking line, lady!"

"He is west of here, far west. The bones speak of salt oceans and high mountains."

"Far west as a man can go?"

Sees All Ways gathered up the fragile slivers of ivory, slowly and carefully. Twice she glanced up at Abe, as though she were thinking of saying something more.

"What?" he asked. "Say it, will you?"

"Trader had other friends, you say. And some are living. Two, or possibly three. I see a woman with hair like living fire and she has the power also. She can 'see' what is there to be seen."

"Krysty Wroth. Other two must be J. B. Dix and Ryan Cawdor."

"The signs tell me of them."

Abe grinned. "Yeah? Come on, old lady, tell me what you see about Ryan and the others."

"I see them in great and terrible danger."

Chapter Ten

The fortress home of the Baron Alferd Nelson stood high on a promontory, accessible only by a narrow two-lane blacktop that had been kept swept clear of snow.

It had once been a resort hotel, built, according to Doc's whispered guesses, around the first third of the twentieth century. It had originally been called the Vista Encantadora Hotel and had been a retirement home for elderly and senior military officers, ending up as a seedier, cheaper motel called, simply, the Vista.

The baron had retained the name when he took it over as the center for his own ville and hunting demesne.

His sec patrol had been out on skis, moving fast and silently across the powdery snow. It was a skill that Ryan had never mastered, though he could get along adequately.

The baron had trained his men well. The ambush had been perfectly and safety executed, with the

warning voice coming unexpectedly from the shadows beneath the trees.

None of the friends moved. Ryan half turned,
glancing over his right shoulder, not seeing anyone. "How do we know you got the guns to take
us all?" he asked quietly.

"You don't. Make the wrong move and it gets
to be corpse-counting day. You can try it."

"Mebbe not."

"You're wise, outlander. You're in some deepish shit, chilling Big Bob like that. Baron Nelson
always fancied taking the mutie demon out himself. Still, deepish shit isn't like being down on
your back, watching the sky out of fading eyes, is
it? Or just the one eye in your case."

The patrol wore hooded white parkas and pants,
making them hard to spot out in the open. They
were all armed with the traditional sec man's favorite weapon of choice, the trusty old M-16 automatic rifle. Technically these were M-16A5s,
chambered to take a standard 9 mm round. The
effective range of the old Army blaster was just
under 350 yards. It could be fired in four modes:
on single shot, semiautomatic, automatic or on full
cyclic. At close to a thousand rounds per minute,
the latter would empty a full 30-round mag in a
breath under two seconds.

The dozen men in the sec squad looked like they

knew how to handle the rifles. Ryan watched them leave cover after he and the others had carefully placed their own blasters on the ground.

"Good. My name's Rick Coburn, outside sec chief to Baron Alferd Nelson of Vista ville." He was tall and skinny, fortyish, with a flattened face and narrowed eyes, and he had a surprisingly gentle voice.

"Any chance of us sort of slip-sliding away, Mr. Coburn," Andy asked deferentially. "As a big favor?"

The sec boss looked at the speaker, his eyes widening a little. "Well, I should've guessed. Been picking up tracks of three men for days now. Crossing and recrossing them. Three men. One with a limp. Andy, Clint No Teeth and Al, the king of the knives."

"We was only intent on moving out through the high pass before the serious snows came, Captain," Clint said.

"Sure. Just happened to take a goat on the baron's land five days ago, then gut-shot an elk a day later. Never even finished it off, did you, boys? Let the poor animal drag her guts through the brush. Got a mind to do exactly the same with you three. Open you up and pull out a loop of your belly. Tether you by it and walk away."

"You wouldn't do that, would you, Cap?" Al asked, his lip twitching nervously.

Coburn ignored him, looking more carefully at the array of firearms in the bloodied dirt. "More to the point—" his eyes raked the group, settling finally on Ryan Cawdor "—is who you seven are and what you're doing with poaching meat thieves like these three."

"We aren't."

"Aren't what, outlander? And I'd like to know some names before we go one freezing breath further with this talk."

"I'm Ryan Cawdor. My friends are Krysty Wroth, Mildred Wyeth, Doc Tanner, J. B. Dix, Michael Brother, and the boy's my son, Dean. Come from the south to do some trading. Hunt. Hire out our blasters now and again. But we don't steal, and we don't go across barons."

Rick Coburn nodded, his face a marble mask of indifference.

"Could be they're hired chillers," Al suggested. "Mebbe like the ones they said went to Vista and—"

"Shut it," Coburn ordered. "Shut it now. Keep it shut." He turned to Ryan again. "Mebbe he got something. There's been trouble at the ville. Serious trouble."

"What kind? Hired guns? Bands of roving wolf's-head outerlaws?"

"Something like that. Best you hear about it from Baron Nelson. I reckon he'll be real interested in you." He paused. "Some of you."

Ryan had been watching the sec men watching them, hoping to see a casual lack of attention that would offer a chance of getting back their weapons and taking out the patrol. But he was disappointed. The men were alert, cold-eyed. Careful.

"If you want these outlanders, Mr. Coburn, then mebbe you could just let us go. Baron won't be wanting us, not when he sees this lot. What do you say, Mr. Coburn?"

"I say you lose your life, you poaching son of a bitch."

He turned to two sec men. "Put them away."

"All of them, sir?"

"No, you dumb fuck. Think I'd be wasting my breath on talking if we were going to whack them all?"

"Those three?"

Coburn nodded, closing his eyes for a moment in exasperation. "Yeah. Those three."

Doc whispered to Mildred, "So difficult to find decent staff these days, wouldn't you say?"

Rick Coburn turned to him. "You want to have

us close your eyes and your mouth, Doc, then just keep on cracking wise like that.''

"Cracking wise!" Mildred exclaimed. "You watch old detective vids, Coburn?"

"Yeah. You?"

"Sure. Chandler, Hammet, Harvey and Leonard and Hillerman. Love them.''

"Chandler? Man who walked along all of those mean streets?''

"And wasn't mean himself. Right.''

The sec boss had been distracted from his flash of anger against Doc, and he turned to his second in command.

"Do them. Leave the dead meat by the body of Big Bob. Sort of visible lesson for anyone who comes out this way.''

"Wolves'll get them first, sir.''

"Yeah.''

As executions went, Ryan had to give Coburn and his men at least an eight from ten.

While most of the patrol kept watch over the seven companions, four of the others took care of the business at hand. They arranged Burne, Kael and Vayre into a ragged line, facing the huge, steaming corpse of the giant mutie grizzly.

Once they'd heard the casual sentence of death, the trio of hunters seemed to lose all their heart and spirit.

Al Vayre had fallen to his knees, hands clasped together, starting to patter a long, barely audible prayer, sounding as if he were trying to admit all of his sins before being propelled in front of the pearly gates.

Clint Kael's head slumped. He'd beckoned to Ryan, who'd been given the nod from Coburn to go and stand by him.

"You might walk from this, mister."

"Who knows? What did you want?"

"Got a daughter and a wife." He hesitated a moment. "Well, last I heard I did. Little girl's name is Paula. Lives out east. Calls herself a New-yorker, but she got a place about fifty miles west of there. Haven't seen much of her. Truth is, the name of Clint don't ring bells in her heart."

"Cut it short," Coburn warned.

Kael nodded. "Just, if you ever get that way, tell her that her daddy went to rest in the arms of Jesus with her name on his lips and her face locked in his heart forever."

"Sure." Ryan saw that the silver-haired man was starting to cry, great crystal tears rolling down his chin and falling into the trodden snow.

"You'll remember?"

"Course." Ryan walked back to rejoin the other six on the far side of the clearing.

"What did he say?" Krysty asked.

"Nothing."

"Nothing?"

"Just empty words. Not worth the trouble of remembering."

Andy Burne had limped away and leaned his hand against the ice-slick bole of a tall ponderosa pine. "Anyone got any jolt?" he asked.

Coburn grinned. "Way to go, huh? No."

"I got some, sir," the youngest of the sec guards offered.

"No." Coburn shook his head. "Don't waste it on a dead man."

"Get to it, then," Burne said. "Time's passing and I feel the cold in this leg."

Michael Brother stepped forward, drawing several M-16 muzzles toward him. "I don't think it's right for you to execute these men without any sort of a trial."

"That right, son? If it is, *son*. Wearing a big girl's dress like that."

"Just for taking game from the forest."

"Forests around here belong to Baron Alferd Nelson, son."

"No man should control or own or use the Earth for private gain," Michael said calmly.

Coburn smiled and stepped in close. Ryan guessed what was about to happen and struggled to avoid interfering.

"You got a swift mouth, son." The right fist of the senior sec man jabbed into Michael's stomach, a savage blow that would have doubled him over, puking in the dirt.

But it never landed.

There was a flicker of movement, so lightning fast that it brought a gasp of amazement from the watching guards. And the teenager was gripping Coburn's right fist in his own right hand.

"No," said the sec officer, warning his patrol. "No problem, guys." He removed his gloved hand from Michael's grasp. "You got faster reflexes than a striking rattler, son."

"I work at it."

"By God, but I bet you do." The narrowed eyes sought Ryan, found him. "You got any other surprises up your sleeve, Cawdor?" The sec boss grinned and shook his head. "Guess you won't answer that, anyway."

"I still tell you that you can have no real right, before God, to murder these men," Michael insisted.

"Let it lie," Ryan called. "No point in this. You made your protest, but it won't change a damned thing here."

"That's right," Coburn said approvingly. "Got some sense for a one-eyed man."

Andy Burne was kicking at a small rock half-buried in the slippery mud. "Can we get this fucking done?"

"Sure." Coburn nodded. "Do them."

A single round for each man was all it took.

Al Vayre pitched forward as though a mule had kicked him in the head. He took two staggering steps, then slumped on the ground, arms and legs spread wide like a dying starfish.

The second bullet from the sec man's blaster was fired at point-blank range at Clint Kael. He was half turning as the gun went off, and the 9 mm slug hit a little to the right of his nape. It angled upward and exited just above the man's left eye, bursting out in a welter of bone and brain tissue that soaked his silver hair.

Kael went down in a heap, his right arm clawing at the frozen earth, fingernails snapping with a brittle sound.

The sec man took a step to one side, bringing his rifle to his shoulder, ready to take out the last of the three hunters.

"Hope you bastards all rot forever in hell," Andy Burne said.

The muzzle-flash set fire to the long hair at the back of his skull, which flared for a moment as he tottered a few steps and collapsed.

"That's it," Rick Coburn announced. "So perish all who steal from the Baron Nelson."

"Words don't make it right, son," Doc said. "They never have, and they never will."

"Guess that's true enough, old-timer. But they're the ones who're down and done."

"Now what?" Krysty said.

"Now we go meet the baron."

Chapter Eleven

The patrol, with their seven prisoners, reached their home turf in a little over two hours. Rick Coburn was a careful man, and he sent a couple of his men out in front, on their skis, breaking trail and keeping a watch out. Then came Ryan and his companions, with the rest of the sec men bringing up the rear.

With no blasters, and on foot against swift experts on skis, they had no hope of escape.

Ryan took the opportunity to walk a ways with each of the others, talking quietly to them about what to do.

And what not to do.

"Keep quiet and easy," he cautioned. "No way of breaking away right now. Don't figure we face too bad a time. Been dead in the snow with the other three if we had. Meet this baron and listen. Think with our ears not our mouths." That part he stressed particularly to his son. "And we watch and wait."

After that he drifted toward the rear of the party

until he was close to the leader of the sec men. Ryan considered Rick Coburn an impressive officer and wanted to try to find a little more from him about where they were going.

And what they might expect there.

"Much farther?" he asked, his voice the only sound above the relentless hissing of the skis through the powdery snow.

"Quarter hour."

"That it up there?" he queried, pointing ahead of them at a great spur of rock that jutted from the flank of the snow-layered mountain.

"Yeah."

A few yards more. It was laborious going, and everyone's breath hung around them like steam from a sauna.

"Coburn?"

"What?"

"What's going on with this baron?"

The slit eyes turned toward him, and something like a smile touched the edges of the knife-blade mouth. "How's that, Cawdor?"

"You don't strike me as a stupid man, Coburn. Most sec bosses get where they are by not being stupid. You know what I mean."

"I know."

"So?"

"Knowing's not the same as telling, outlander. You understand that."

"I have a responsibility for everyone in my group—a kid, a teenager, two women and an old man."

"And two of the meanest coldheart bastards I ever saw. You and the little guy with the glasses, Cawdor." Coburn laughed, barking like a fox. "Don't play the hearts and flowers with me. Won't bring the watery pearls to my eyes for you."

Ryan smiled, instinctively liking the tough sec man. The brutal executions hadn't bothered him at all. Burne, Kael and Vayre knew the game they were playing, knew the risks of losing.

And knew the price paid by losers throughout all of Deathlands.

"You could still tell me what's been going down with the baron and why it might affect us."

Coburn trudged on, shaking his head. "No. Baron Nelson's not what you'd exactly call a forgiving man, Cawdor."

"Never met a baron who was strong on the forgiving side."

"Bet your ass on that! Triple ace on the line, outlander."

Ryan picked his way forward again to walk with Krysty.

"He tell you anything, lover?"

"I've seen clams with looser lips."

"Says something about this Baron Nelson. He must be a big man."

Krysty was right, in more ways than one.

ONCE THEY REACHED the defense perimeter of the ville's headquarters, Coburn relaxed a little. He sent most of the patrol off-duty, ordering them to carry all of the strangers' captured weapons to the armory.

The Vista was in surprisingly good shape. It had been freshly painted and had its own water-turbo power plant, from the river that surged behind it. There was a main lobby area, which seemed to have been built from giant redwood tree trunks, some of them over fifteen feet in circumference.

Armed guards were everywhere, carrying automatic rifles.

"You get many threats from outside?" J.B. asked.

"Not often. Not until..." Coburn hesitated as though he knew he'd been on the verge of saying more than he'd intended.

"No wars with another baron?"

Coburn looked at Ryan, his face suddenly tight with suspicion. "Why do you ask that?"

"Happens. Never met a baron slept easy at night

or didn't look back over his shoulder ten times every minute."

"Baron Nelson defeated the man who ruled here. Long time ago. He died. But his son lives and leads a pack of hired raiders. Homeless bastard dogs."

Coburn's voice held a cold venom that raised the hackles at the back of Ryan's neck.

"This man have a name?" he asked.

"Sure. Good name. Sidler. Calls himself Wizard. Got half a dozen men, is all." He sounded bitter, but a note of grudging respect had crept into his voice. "Good at what they do. Rape, burning, torture and chilling."

A woman appeared at the balcony of the gallery that ran around the entrance hall, rang a small silver bell and beckoned to Coburn.

"Baron's ready," she called. "Says to bring them up to his rooms."

"Not a good idea to keep him waiting," the sec boss said.

Chapter Twelve

The room had the same rough-hewn-timber look as the rest of the fortress. Heavy shutters were folded back from the windows, revealing a beautiful view of picturesque mountains.

A log fire blazed in the enormous hearth, and a brindled hound lay asleep on a bearskin rug. A long desk in dark polished wood stood in one corner, and several chairs were scattered around; a tall grandfather clock ticked sonorously close to a half-open door that led through to what Ryan figured must be the baron's sleeping quarters; a walnut gun rack stood against the long wall of the room, holding a variety of good quality blasters—three hunting rifles and half a dozen pump-action shotguns, as well as a shelf of blue-steel automatic pistols.

Two paintings hung in the room. One showed a great stag, standing at bay among misty hills, facing its unseen pursuers with a stubborn grandeur. The other was a good ten feet long and four feet high. At first it seemed to show only a turbulent fall of foaming, peat-colored water in a rainy, dull landscape of weathered moors. But as Ryan stepped across the patterned carpet, the overhead light glinted off the picture, showing a tiny flash of gold and silver in the midst of the frozen torrent. A salmon had been caught by the artist in the midst of its climactic leap for life.

"Stand here and wait," Coburn said quietly. "And take some advice. Ears open and mouths closed. Best that way."

A scent of tobacco lingered in the room, as though the baron smoked a pipe. In the far chamber they could all hear the muffled sound of organ music, ponderous and deep.

"Bach's *Toccata and Fugue*," Mildred whispered, attracting a glare from Rick Coburn.

The door opened wider and a small woman came slowly in. She was of average height and build, with a mane of pure white hair that tumbled to her waist. Tiny yellow and white flowers were threaded through its unbrushed length.

She looked to be about sixty, with a pale face and nervous, darting eyes. Her pale slender fingers tangled in front of her as though they were wrestling with one another.

"My lady," the sec boss said, lowering his head in a bow.

She smiled vaguely at him and sat on an embroidered chaise longue near the fire. Ryan noticed that her feet were bare.

"Dowager mother of Baron Nelson," Coburn whispered out of the corner of his mouth.

Ryan figured that the old lady was at least two cards short of an inside straight.

There was movement in the far room, and the doorway was filled by the figure of the baron of Vista ville, Colorado.

Alferd Nelson.

Like his mother, he had hair that was as white and pure as wind-washed snow, and a long beard to go with it. At a quick guesstimate, Ryan thought that the baron was several inches over seven feet tall. But he wasn't skinny and frail. His shoulders were broad, his chest deep, and he probably weighed in around three hundred pounds.

Alferd Nelson wore a russet woolen jerkin over dark green corduroy pants, tucked into polished brown knee-high boots. On his right hip in a hand-tooled Texas rig he carried a pearl-handled Smith & Wesson Magnum with a ten-inch barrel. On his left hip the baron wore a sheathed cavalry saber with a brass hilt.

Ryan wasn't a man to be easily impressed, but he had to admit that Baron Nelson was an impressive figure.

But there was something else, beyond the massive size.

Dean identified it first, tugging his father's sleeve and whispering very quietly, "Doesn't he look sad?"

The lined face that turned slowly to look along the row of seven strangers was tainted with the deepest misery.

"These are the outlanders who are responsible for ending the magnificent life of Big Bob, are they not, Mr. Coburn?"

"That's right, Baron."

"Why are they here?"

"Baron?"

The leonine head turned toward the sec boss. "You aren't usually slow in the brain, Mr. Coburn. It was a simple question."

"You mean why didn't I have them chilled out in the woods?"

"Yes. Poachers and intruders into my lands know what to expect."

Doc coughed. "If I may say so, Baron, that's a crassly arrogant and pompous statement. Typical of the way that all power corrupts and absolute power corrupts absolutely."

Baron Nelson looked once in his direction, then turned back to Rick Coburn, as though the old man hadn't spoken.

"I pay you, Mr. Coburn, to be the cleansing wind that purges darkness from this place. We know how bitter and infinite that darkness can be. Do we not, Mr. Coburn?"

"Yeah, Baron. Guess you haven't heard all the news yet. These seven aren't from around here. They were with three others who—"

"Livestock and game have been slaughtered."

"Not by them."

"Big Bob?"

"Uh, yeah, Baron. They took him out all right. But they—"

A weary hand raised. "I don't wish to hear. Take them out and hang them."

"The women and kid as well?"

For the first time since he'd entered the large room, Baron Alferd Nelson showed some sort of positive reaction.

"Women and a child. I hadn't bothered to notice that, Mr. Coburn."

Ryan decided that it was time to speak. "Can I say something, Baron?"

"Why not? Your name is…"

"Ryan Cawdor. Years back I was the son of Baron Titus Cawdor of the ville of Front Royale over east in the Shens."

"Now you come here to hunt down the largest grizzly that Deathlands has ever known. A mutie animal bigger than anything that the..." He lost the sentence, and his words trailed away into the stillness. Near the fire, his mother suddenly sneezed.

Coburn shuffled his feet, glancing sideways at Ryan, half closing one eye in something that might have been a wink of support.

Or might not.

The baron gathered his thoughts. "You were hired to kill Big Bob," he said. "To take his head and his hide and sell it to someone. Who was the man behind your blasters, Cawdor?"

"Nobody. We were moving through. Didn't know we were on anyone's land. Saw tracks of the grizzly. Knew that it was a big son of a bitch animal. Next thing we know we're on a trail by a river and it's rushing us. Could've chilled any of us. All of us. So we whacked it."

"We didn't want to chill it," Krysty added. "Not something as magnificent as that. But it was the bear or us."

Now the huge man was interested. "What wonderful hair you have. And your name is..."

"Krysty, Baron. Krysty Wroth, late of the ville of Harmony."

"You say you had no choice in taking Big Bob to animal heaven?"

"No choice."

"Mr. Coburn?" The baron turned questioningly to the sec boss.

"Way it looked, the grizzly came charging at them. If they were after it for a trophy, they'd have tracked it and picked it off real careful. Reckon they put close on fifty rounds into it."

The baron laughed, quickly cutting it off. "It would take that much to stop Big Bob, I believe."

"Ask them." The voice came from the ghostly figure of the old lady.

"Later, mother."

"Now."

"I said I would ask them later."

"Ask them now, Alferd."

"No, Mother."

She stood, her milky eyes wandering across the group. "Then I will ask them."

"No, you will not."

The baron took three long strides, towering over the white-haired woman. She shrank from his glaring anger.

"Don't strike me, Alferd. Not in the face, sweetheart."

"Keep your mouth shut, woman! I decide what'll be told and what questions will be asked in Vista. Me and me alone!"

"But he was such a sweet child, Alferd."

"And she was a good woman. A good woman

turned whore-slut, Mother. I don't grieve for her passing, but the boy…''

Now the puzzle was becoming a little clearer to Ryan, the sec patrols and the triple-careful defenses around the ville. Something had happened to the baron's child.

"Son or daughter?" he asked Baron Nelson.

"A son, outlander. I will tell you something of it, here and now. It was three months ago, in the days of summer sun."

Chapter Thirteen

Zebe Nelson had been eight days past his eleventh birthday, and was the only living child of Baron Alferd and his woman, Clare.

The boy was tall for his age, already close to six feet. He was good-looking, apart from a slight squint in his left eye. Zebe had his mother's reddish hair and pale complexion.

Vista ville hadn't suffered any serious trouble from Wizard Sidler over at Yuma for better than three years.

There was an occasional raiding party and a burning up on the northeast side of Nelson's land, some cattle taken before the fall roundup, and a couple of good hands butchered one July morning in a line shack beyond the river.

Zebe was very keen on fishing and was sometimes allowed to go after trout at Silverhead Lake, up a broad valley eight miles west of Vista. Well within the safe area.

"Well within the safe area," Baron Nelson repeated, leaning his arm on the mantel, staring broodingly into the flames.

Coburn spoke softly. "Got zones. Green in and around the ville itself. Moves to yellow when you get two miles off. Orange after ten miles and then red for another ten miles. After that you're going into the unclaimed lands, and you might easy find a Yuma patrol on your back."

"Silverhead Lake's safe," the baron insisted. "Wouldn't have let the boy go without a full sec patrol if it had been dangerous. Never guessed that those trappers were paid by Sidler. They ate our fucking food and drank our fucking drink and slept in our fucking beds." He paused, drawing in a long, trembling breath through pursed lips. "And one of them fucked my fucking wife."

"Now you don't know that, Alferd," his mother said reproachfully.

"I didn't see his snake dick slipping between her legs, Mother. But I saw the snail trail on her thighs and the smile on her lips and felt the warmth of the sheets."

Nobody spoke. By now the seven companions had been allowed to sit, listening to the anguished story.

Alferd Nelson had killed the sluttish young wife that he believed had betrayed him with one, or all, of the six trappers.

By the time he discovered his wife's infidelity, the visitors had gone.

Gone up to Silverhead Lake.

"To do the job they'd been sent on," the sec boss stated.

The baron walked unsteadily to a side table, opening the cupboard beneath it. He took out a round goblet of hand-cut crystal and a matching decanter, three-quarters full with brandy. He poured himself a large measure and gulped it.

The baron spun around to look at the others in the room, taking a step back so quickly that he slurped half the liquor onto the carpet. "What are you boggling at, like a string of death watchers?"

"You were telling us about your son's murder," Mildred reminded him gently.

"Yes. About the murder of my son."

Rick Coburn had been the first up to the lakeside, leading ten of his best sec men, searching for the eleven-year-old boy when he and his two guards hadn't returned for the evening meal.

The sun had been setting, and a monstrous chem storm had been threatening from the direction of old Denver. Thunderheads towered over the surrounding mountains, and already the first tracery of vivid silver lightning was visible.

Zebe Nelson's escorts had been murdered, both men shot several times with high-velocity rifles.

Their corpses had been stripped naked and mutilated with narrow-bladed flensing knives.

"Recognized Josef from a bobcat scar on his shoulder. Trace went out with Josef, so we figured that the second body had to be his. Wasn't any way of telling. Trace's mother wouldn't have known him. The way they did it, but couldn't even tell if it was a man or a woman lying on the pebbles."

Coburn walked to the window and stood looking out, reaching up to touch his face as though he'd gotten something in his eye.

The baron picked up the story, draining his glass and looking at it in a puzzled manner, as if someone else had sneaked up and drunk it away from under his nose. He pivoted and hurled it down into the hearth, where it smashed into a thousand bright splinters of glass.

"Took longer to find my son." He sighed, shaking his head. "He was only eleven."

Dean glanced across the warm room at his father, but said nothing.

Coburn had spread his men out.

They knew that the trappers had left the ville hours earlier. The death of Alferd's wife had been a fair guide to the timing, as had the cold rigor of the hacked flesh of the two corpses.

"I found him," the sec boss said, turning away from the window.

Coburn had made a hesitant effort to conceal the facts from the baron, but nobody got to be in charge of a large ville without being able to read the faces of the men who worked for him.

Alferd Nelson had insisted on every vile detail of the way his only child had been tortured before an agonized and prolonged passing. And he'd examined for himself, alone in the small chapel of Vista, the mangled remains of the boy.

"They went to this ville of Yuma?" J.B. asked. "The place of this man called Sidler?"

"Correct," the baron replied.

"How long ago?"

"Three months, is it not, Mr. Coburn? Or is it four?"

"Nearer five, Baron."

"Ah, yes. Time passes so quickly when you are having pleasure. My father used to say that, you know. How grossly, appallingly lacking in truth it is. For me, with my only child gone—my son and heir—time stands still."

J.B. persisted with his questions. He had picked up a small china figure of a beaver and was holding it between finger and thumb. "Any names for these trappers? Anyone we might possibly have heard of?'' He turned to Coburn for the answer when the baron ignored him.

The sec boss rubbed the back of his hand across his chin. ''We list all outlanders that come to the ville. Have their names someplace. There were six, now I recall it. One called Grant. Another called Julio, or some kind of Mex name.'' He paused. ''Have to check them, in case any of you've come across them in your journeying. Oh, yeah. Third one was called Jennison.''

''There was a small sound as J.B. fumbled the little porcelain beaver and dropped it on the floor, where it broke into three pieces.

''Sorry,'' he said, stooping to pick it up.

Nelson's mother smiled graciously at him. ''Let it lie. I never liked the ugly thing.''

The baron lifted a hamlike hand. ''Heard you all got some good blasters with you, and some of you look like you might know how to use them. I got a plan sort of bubbling away in my mind. How you can help me and I can help you. Got to think about it some.''

Ryan's experience of barons and their plans for ''helping'' you was that the balance of ''help'' generally lay pretty heavily on their side.

''The boy looks something of the age of Zebe, Mr. Cawdor. There is a resemblance to you.''

It wasn't clear whether there was a question hidden in there. Ryan nodded. "My son, Baron. Yeah, he's just eleven years old."

"Smaller than Zebe. Then again, you are a smaller man than I am. My dear dead wife was tall for a woman. Zebe will be very tall when—" He stopped and suddenly looked carefully at his fingers, as if he were examining them for specks of blood. "Of course he won't get any taller now. Mr. Cawdor, have you lost someone you loved?"

"More times than I can count, Baron."

The great head nodded slowly, the mane of white hair concealing the deep-set eyes. "Then you know why I feel I must... When a bullet has been fired, it is a foolish man who does not immediately replace it with another round in the magazine. Do you not all agree with me?" Nobody spoke. "Well, you do not seem to disagree. That is what I believe."

He lapsed into a silence so long that the sec boss eventually broke it. "What do you want me to do with them, Baron?"

"Do with them? Why, bring them to the evening meal in one hour's time, Mr. Coburn. Bring all of them. The women. And the child. All of them."

Chapter Fourteen

"My mother sends her regrets that she's unable to dine with us. She is old and frail, and finds life is sometimes too much for her these gloomy days."

Baron Alferd Nelson had already made a similar apology for the dowager three times during the meal. And they were still only at the beginning of the meat course.

Considering his enormous, near-mutie size, the ruler of Vista ville had an extraordinarily poor head for alcohol.

There had been a dry white wine served with the soup and fish, and now a rich deep maroon merlot with the fricassee of pork and sweet potatoes. For those who preferred it, there were brimming flagons of locally brewed beer.

The table was a good twenty feet long, made from a single polished slab of veined redwood. The cutlery was pewter, dating back from before the long winters. The glass was as fine as anything that Ryan had ever seen, cut with patterns of intertwined acanthus and vine leaves. Dean was fascinated by the way that the heavy goblets rang when he tapped on them with his finger.

Nelson sat at the head, wearing a loose shirt of white linen, hanging outside black cord pants. Ryan had noticed immediately that both the blaster and the saber were conspicuously in place.

The baron had drained the first glass of the Chablis in a single gulp, wiping his mouth with the back of a hand, glowering around the table.

"Welcome, guests," he'd said without any hint of irony.

Dean had been placed at his right elbow, with Krysty on the left. Ryan sat next to her, Mildred on his left. Michael was next to Dean, J.B. along the table from him. Doc was last in the line, sitting opposite the taciturn sec boss, Rick Coburn. Half a dozen of his men stood discreetly around the room, their automatic M-16s at the ready.

The food was excellent, the wines unusually rich on the palate. Conversation was halting as nobody knew what was going on, or what was in the baron's mind.

Alferd Nelson's mood swings became more erratic as the meal wore on. He seemed fascinated with Dean Cawdor, offering the boy more wine, which he kept refusing, taking note of his father's warning signals. But the baron also cut up choice pieces of the salmon, giving it to the lad off his own fork.

Ryan kept a careful watch.

In different circumstances he'd have placed an obvious interpretation on Nelson's behavior toward his young son. But it didn't seem to be at all sexual, just a delighted preoccupation that appeared to have its roots in the recent loss of his own eleven-year-old boy.

He kept asking what hobbies and interests Dean had. "Fishing?"

"Sometimes."

"Hunting?"

"When I'm hungry."

Baron Nelson laughed at that. "Shooting. Zebe was good with a bow or a rifle."

"I'm not bad with a rifle. Not that great with a bow and arrows."

Another glass of the rich red wine vanished, and Alferd Nelson clapped the boy on the shoulder, nearly knocking him from his chair.

"You and I can go fishing every day, when the summer comes once more and the ice vanishes from the creeks. How about that?"

Dean looked at his father, who shrugged imperceptibly. Nelson was as drunk as a skunk, and getting drunker by the minute. Another thing that experience taught you about surviving in Deathlands was that it wasn't generally a good idea to argue with a drunken baron.

"Yeah," the boy said cautiously.

"We staying here, Baron?" Michael asked, grinning woozily.

"Perhaps. Some are and some aren't. Some will and some won't. What do you say to that, young… Michael, isn't it?"

"It is, Baron. What do I say?" The teenager laid his head down on the table, blinking and smiling. "I'd say that my face looks like the rising sun, doesn't it?"

Drink had made him flushed. Baron Nelson reached out an enormous arm and ruffled the young man's hair. "You shall have better clothes, Master Rising Sun. Real clothes."

"I like these, Baron." The youth sat up, his voice rising in anger.

Ryan interrupted. "Been thinking for some time you should dress safer, Michael. Take up the baron on his kind offer."

The snap of warning in his voice penetrated the youngster's befuddled mind and he nodded. "Oh, right. Yeah. Sure, Ryan, I understand. Clothes. Pants, shirts and stuff."

"And some boots for those fare beet," Nelson said. "I mean bare feet. Bear's neat. Hairy meat. Mary's sweet."

Reaching for one of the dark green bottles of wine, the baron knocked it over with his sleeve, sending a cascade of deep crimson across the snow cloth and staining it like a butcher's apron.

"A fearful omen, perhaps," Nelson observed, shaking his head. "Zebe was so pale, you know. What they did drained every last drop of blood from his little body."

"You have to go on living, Baron," Krysty said. "Either you stand still and give up, or you carry on best you can."

"You think so, Krysty?"

"You stand still, then you find that you're sitting down. Next moment you realize that you're lying flat on your back, then they're shovelling in the wet clay."

"Krysty Wroth is about the wisest person I ever met, Baron," Doc said. "I have personally been bereaved in, believe it or not, an even more brutal way than you."

"Impossible, old doctor." Now he'd reached another bottle and had filled his glass to the brim again. "Impossible."

"My dear wife Emily. My little cherub, Rachel, barely three years old, and the tiny seraph, Jolyon, in his first year of life. Each of them plucked away in a single head-splitting moment. You lost a wife

and a son, Baron. I was fated to go one better."
Doc laughed bitterly. "One worse."

Alferd Nelson gestured with the glass, spilling
more of the merlot. "Grief cannot be measured in
ones, twos or threes, my friend. I listen to your
words, but I don't hear them. I look at you but I
don't see you."

Doc nodded. "Truly said. But it does nothing to
diminish Krysty's words. The canker in your heart
can be excised only by time. You can do nothing
to bring your little boy back to you."

The glass flew across the room, showering one
of the sec men with its red spray. It struck a hanging tapestry and smashed into a thousand pieces on
the stone floor.

Nelson was on his feet, pounding the table with
a huge fist, making the cutlery jump and rattle.
"Wrong!" he bellowed. "That is where you are
wrong, Doctor."

"What do you mean, Baron?" Ryan asked, suddenly wishing he had the SIG-Sauer cocked and
ready in his hand.

"The good doctor is wrong, my one-eyed outlander friend."

"Wrong? How's he wrong?"

"Said that I couldn't do anything to bring Zebe
back. Revenge hasn't been possible for me, and
those scum still live, eat and sleep. Only a couple

of days' march from here in Yuma. Under the gloved hand of Sidler.''

J.B. tried to interrupt the raging monologue.

"Baron, we—"

"I knew that an idea would come to me. Kill two birds in the same bush.''

"Why not just go and raid Yuma and hang the men who killed your boy?'' The Armorer lifted his voice, penetrating through the wraith of blind anger that gripped Alferd Nelson.

"Ah, there is the question. *The* question. J. B. Dix asks it. A man who I look at and see a small person, not overstrong, wearing spectacles. Mild seeming man. But I see beyond that, Mr. Dix. I see someone who knows about death and its infinite ways. Your question strikes at the core of what happened. Why do I not raid Yuma?''

"You got the men.''

"Indeed, Mr. Dix. I have the men. Good men. And Mr. Coburn is as good a sec boss as you'd find in a month's journeys. Tell them, Mr. Coburn, why my son's death is not avenged.''

"Sure, Baron. Vista is a strong fortress. Easy to defend and double difficult to attack. Yuma is worse. One way in and out. Not got the discipline we have here, but they got more men. Twice the men. Three times. It's like an old hole-in-the-wall sort of den of thieves and killers. Some crap-poor blasters, but a lot of them. They can't hope to take Vista ville without limitless losses.''

''And you can't go against Yuma, mob-handed, for the same reason,'' J.B. said, nodding. ''I can see that.''

''So send in a small raiding party,'' Dean suggested. ''Chill them.''

Nelson leaned across and kissed him on the cheek. To his credit the boy sat still, resisting the temptation to pull away.

''You are a fine and brave lad,'' the baron said. ''And you have shone your little light into the dark place that I have been trying to illuminate. But I have not had the right tools for my purpose.'' He strode to the door. ''Coburn!''

''Baron?''

''Allow our visitors to finish their meal. Convey them to sleeping quarters and watch them well. Watch them very well. And bring Ryan Cawdor to my rooms at eleven o'clock tonight.''

The door slammed behind him.

Chapter Fifteen

They hadn't stayed long over the remnants of the meal, though Michael had insisted on having a third helping of a delicious cherry cobbler with fresh cream.

Before showing them to their sleeping quarters, Rick Coburn had reminded Ryan about some new clothes for the teenager.

"Baron was drunk when he suggested that to me," Michael said. "I'd rather stick with what I have, though they're sort of torn and dirty, I guess. What do you think, Ryan?"

"I reckon that someone like Baron Nelson might just remember what he said, drunk or sober. Wouldn't want to upset him, Michael."

"Good advice," the sec man agreed. "Come see what we got."

There was a storeroom beneath the main eating area, vaulted and cold. Coburn took Ryan and the teenager quickly from section to section, pulling out racks of shirts, pants and boots.

Michael shook his head. "I really don't want to

change the way I dress, Ryan. It's like giving up another part of my past. A big part of it. Do I really have to go through with this?''

''Yeah. Look, it's cold enough to freeze the milk in a seal's tit out there. And your bare feet'll finish getting you…getting all of us into real trouble one day.''

''What kind? I never had a problem, and I've been going barefoot more or less since I became an oblate up at Nil-Vanity. Since I was a little kid, hardly walking.''

Coburn laughed. ''I been places that even hand-stitched combat boots, good-quality, got ripped and torn. Devil's Dance Floor, on the southern edge of the old Badlands.''

''Yeah.'' Ryan grinned. ''I been there. And up on Knife-edge Crest. In the Sangre de Cristo Mountains. Jagged spurs of rock. Saw a mule stumble and go over onto one. Went right in one side and out the other, like a great spear.''

''And there's thorns,'' Coburn continued, winking at Ryan behind the young man's back. ''Eighteen inches long, barbed, with enough poison to take out a regiment of stickies.''

''And chiggers. Little crimson grubs that burrow in between the toes. Crawl up the inside of the veins in both your legs.'' Ryan grinned back at the tall sec boss.

"Up your legs, then lay their eggs in your balls. Hundreds of them come sliding out the end of your cock. Nasty, son."

Michael wrinkled his face in disgust. "I think you're pulling my leg, but I get the message. Yes, I see."

He picked heavy-duty black jeans, with narrow silver piping and copper rivets. The shirt he chose was also black denim, with a warm thermal lining. He added a quilted vest and a thick winter parka. All in black.

"Try these. Real good boots," Ryan suggested. "And a couple of pairs of wool socks. These boots lace up to the knee. Your color, too. Black. Trekking boots, Michael. Walk anywhere in them."

The teenager took the bundle and headed for one of the narrow changing cubicles that lined the hewn-stone walls.

"Sure. I could walk anywhere before."

But he rather fancied the image he saw reflected in the flyblown mirror by the door. Ryan was impressed with the stocky, muscular figure.

"Better," he said.

"Not so bad," the teenager agreed reluctantly. "Not so bad."

DURING THE TIME before eleven o'clock, the companions discussed what Baron Alferd Nelson was going to talk about to Ryan.

There was a consensus that it wasn't likely to be overwhelmingly good news for them.

At ten forty-five Ryan called the conversation to a halt, while he ticked off on his fingers the points that they'd all agreed on.

"Killed his wife. Could be looking for someone to take her place. Certainly showed some interest in both Mildred and Krysty."

"Haven't seen many women around the ville," Krysty commented.

"Servers and sec wives," J.B. agreed. "Not breeding stock for an ambitious and proud man like Nelson."

"Then that's one thing. But I figure the death of his son—what was his name?"

"Zebe," Dean replied.

"Right, thanks. Zebe. Chilled in a swift and evil-hearted way by this gang of men from Yuma who were under orders from Wizard Sidler." Ryan looked around at the others. "What a name! These killers. We know nothing about them, do we? No? J.B.?"

"What?"

"Sorry. Thought you were going to say something then."

"No."

"Right. The boy. I have this gut feeling that Baron Nelson mainly wants to talk to me about the death of his kid."

Mildred half lifted a hand to attract his attention. "Shouldn't we be thinking of doing a runner and getting out of this place?"

"We got knives against their blasters. And it's a well-run ville, Mildred. Coburn's one of the best sec bosses I ever seen."

"Saw, lover. Best you ever saw."

"Yeah. Best sec boss I ever *saw*. So, we have to wait and see what cards get laid on the table. And play them the best we can."

"At least we won't have to wait very much longer to ascertain his desires," Doc said. "Another few minutes, and you'll be summoned into the august royal presence once more."

ALFERD NELSON WAS SITTING on the sofa in his living room. The fire had sunk to fragile peaks of gray ash, with an occasional winking glow of red embers among them.

The baron was wearing a long, deep purple caftan that was embroidered with swirling patterns in gold and silver thread.

He had a tall, slender glass in his hand, half-filled with a cinnamon-colored liqueur. As Coburn ushered Ryan into the room, Nelson gestured toward a padded armchair across from the hearth.

"Leave us, Mr. Coburn."

"Sure you'll be..."

"I am certain. If the outlander proves troublesome, I shall simply pick him up in one hand and snap him across my knee like a dead branch. Is that right, Cawdor?"

"Sure is, Baron."

Despite the fact that the older man was more than seven feet tall, Ryan would have backed himself in hand-to-hand combat against him. His experience was that really big men were generally slow and clumsy with poor combat reflexes.

Coburn stared at Ryan through his narrowed, almost Oriental eyes, but his expression gave nothing of his feelings. Then he closed the door and left the two men alone together.

"A glass of this excellent spirit, Mr. Cawdor? I recommend it."

"What is it?"

"I call it Victory Vista. It is distilled over near Telluride from honey and grain, with various herbs and spices."

"Sure, why not, Baron?"

"Help yourself. The decanter is on that table."

The long-necked jug was only a third full. Ryan tipped out a small measure into one of the set of glasses on the silver tray. He sipped cautiously at the liqueur, finding it rather too sweet and sticky for his taste, the spices cloying his palate. But it was strong and fiery, and it warmed him as it worked its way into his stomach.

"Sit down, Cawdor."

"Thanks."

"You've been well treated here in my ville?"

"No complaints."

"Good."

"Though I'd like to have our blasters returned to us."

"Perhaps. Perhaps very soon. Depending on how we agree tonight."

"Agree, Baron?"

The lines of bitterness and grief were accentuated by the dim lighting in the room, making Nelson look a hundred years old. Ryan sipped again at the Victory Vista.

But the sweetness lay heavy in his throat, with the acrid harshness of bile.

"Agree with what I am about to say to you. Let us be clear, Cawdor. Mr. Coburn tells me that he believes you and your party are people of violence. I understand that. But what I have decided is not subject to much discussion."

"You mean it's a threat and a promise, all rolled up into one?"

"You take your men to Yuma and bring back the curs who killed my son. I will hold your women and child. If you don't come back, with prisoners, I will take the women to wife and adopt your boy as my own son."

"And that's it, Baron?" Ryan asked.

"That's it."

Chapter Sixteen

"You agreed to this?" Mildred walked away from Ryan, thin-lipped with the intensity of her rage. "You agreed with that fucking beanstalk! I don't believe this, Ryan. You tell us that the odds are stacked against you, J.B., Doc or Michael coming back here safe."

"That's true."

"So that power-crazed snow-headed maniac then decides he'll fuck me and Krysty and use us like brood mares? And your son...*your* son, Ryan, gets to be *his* son."

"That's true as well, Mildred."

"Well, by God, I've heard some triple-stupe things said and seen some triple-stupe things done since I woke up in Deathlands, but this takes the cake."

"What would you have done, Mildred?" Ryan asked quietly.

"I'd have told him to take a flying fuck at a rolling doughnut." She turned to where J.B. was sitting at a small table, patiently greasing and reassembling the Uzi and the Smith & Wesson M-4000 12-gauge, carefully lining up the eight rounds, each containing twenty of the inch-long fléchettes—the tiny darts.

"What?" he asked, realizing that Mildred was looking at him.

"You went along with this, John." She shook her head, the tiny beaded plaits clattering against one another. "Surely we could have gotten together. Chilled a guard. Got weapons. Set a fire. Blown the place apart. Something!"

Doc coughed. "I am aware that you and I have often failed to see eye to eye, my dear Dr. Wyeth. And I do not always agree with what our beloved leader, Ryan Cawdor, says and does." He gripped the lapels of his coat as though he were addressing a faculty meeting at Harvard. "But it seems we are subject to force majeure here. Massively outnumbered and outgunned. From what I have seen of this man, Nelson—" Mildred started to speak, but he held up a hand. "Allow me to finish, if you please. From what I've seen, he is not a rational being. Had Ryan refused, then I think that he and I and Michael, and John Barrymore Dix would all be dead by now. And you and Krysty and the boy would be facing a future so bleak that it wounds the core of my heart to think on it. Do you not see this, Mildred? Do you not?"

It was the longest speech that any of them had ever heard the old man make.

Mildred stared at him, unblinking, for twenty heartbeats. Then she stepped forward and put her arms around him.

"Yeah, Doc," she said. "Yeah."

THEY'D AGREED to leave at dawn.

"Ten days, Mr. Cawdor. You are either back with your prisoners by dawn on the eleventh day, or you need not return at all."

Ryan had argued over a couple of points. He'd wanted to leave both Doc and Michael behind at the ville, insisting that they would slow down J.B. and himself and were both lacking experience in the sort of expedition they were planning.

"No," the baron replied. "They go."

"Six men murdered the boy."

"And Wizard Sidler, who paid them the jack and who sharpened the blades."

"You know we can't hope, however well it goes, to bring seven men back here. Not keeping all of them alive, Baron."

The deep-set eyes looked at him for a long moment. "I am not a cruel man by nature. I want all seven. To punish them. But I do not think of myself as unfair. What you say is true. But I will have my blood! Sidler and two others. Or four from the remaining six. Is that just, Cawdor?"

"Have to be."

KRYSTY AND RYAN SHARED a single bed in the sleeping quarters on the third floor. They had a narrow balcony that looked out over a sliver of frozen lake and the distant mountains, the snow glittering under a hunter's moon.

The fortress was heated from a boiler in the rumbling depths of the basement, pumping hot water around a system of metal pipes. But it was archaic and temperamental and, even working full-bore, it still struggled to keep the ambient temperature up to forty degrees.

Krysty stood looking over the balcony, and her breath plumed out in the silvery air. She was wearing only her shirt and a brief pair of bikini pants.

"You coming back from this one, lover?" she asked softly.

"If I do, then I will."

"Gaia! Don't get all runic and mysterious on me now."

He sat up in bed. "Going to a hostile ville. Got to take old Doc and young Michael with us, then bring some stone-eyed killers back here through winter snows. What can I tell you, Krysty?"

She turned around and he could see that the cold

had stiffened her nipples, straining at the thin material of her T-shirt.

"Guess I wait. Men must work and women must wait. Uncle Tyas McCann used to say that like it was some old truth, carved in marble. But he was right, wasn't he?"

"Watch out for the boy, Krysty." He beckoned to her. "And yourself. Mildred can look after herself. Come to bed."

"You don't get back, then Baron Nelson goes to catch the last train west."

"Wouldn't have expected anything different." She walked slowly across the room, her body shimmering in the dimness, her hair filled with flickering points of fiery light. "If it comes to the sticking point, lover, then try Coburn. Seems a decent man. Might not help you, but he might not come right out and stand in your path."

She pulled back the blanket and slid in beside him, making him gasp as she put her cold feet against his legs. "I'll remember that, Ryan," she whispered. "Right now, I think I'd like to be warmed up."

"No rest from your incessant demands is there?" he said, grinning in the darkness.

"No."

Her long, strong fingers crabbed across his chest, pausing at the puckered knife scar beneath the heart, moving lower, slower, over the flat muscular slab of his stomach and touching the first curling tendrils of thick black hair. They hesitated for a tantalizing moment, then gripped him, squeezing hard enough to make Ryan draw in his breath.

"Sure you're ready for my incessant demands, lover? Oh, I believe you are."

Ryan rolled on his side and kissed her on the cheek, edging around, until he found Krysty's mouth. Their tongues touched, teasing each other, then thrusting harder. He could feel her breasts, peaked against his chest, and he reached down.

"Oh, yes, lover." She sighed, as his fingers entered her.

With a twist of her athlete's body, Krysty wriggled clear around, clambering astride him, facing down his body. Ryan found his head gripped between her powerful thighs, his mouth pressed against her warm, moist sex. He flicked out his tongue, feeling Krysty's instant response.

She leaned forward, hands slithering along his thighs, her long hair tingling over his groin. Then her soft lips closed around him, sucking him into her mouth.

He moaned, but his voice was muffled by her body, and he moved his head from side to side.

It was so arousing that Ryan could feel himself racing toward his climax, and he concentrated on holding back, trying to wait for her. He reached up and used his hands to assist his tongue, aware of the butterfly quivering starting deep within her.

Holding back.

Holding.

"Fireblast!" Though the word exploded only inside his own head.

His back arched as though he were suffering a massive electric shock, and he pushed his hips up toward Krysty's face, feeling the unstoppable surge of power, jetting from him. She locked her arms behind his thighs, pressing herself down onto him. So that they climaxed, locked immovably together.

AN HOUR LATER Ryan was tall in the saddle of a cantankerous skewbald, heading along a narrow trail with J.B., Doc and Michael.

Toward Yuma, Colorado.

Chapter Seventeen

Ryan had spent an hour with Rick Coburn, drawing from the sec boss all the information he could about Yuma and Wizard Sidler.

There was a sketch map, showing the region around the enemy ville, and the maze of small tracks and roads that snaked through the nearby mountains, ending in the single blacktop that was, effectively, the only way in and out.

"Don't know much about the layout there," Coburn admitted.

He told Ryan that Sidler's headquarters was established in an old cinema. His estimate of the number of guns there ranged from twenty to a hundred.

"Fifty might be about right," Coburn said. "Far as we know, the six killers are still up in Yuma. Hope for your sake they haven't moved on."

"Anything else we could know?" Ryan asked.

The sec boss shook his head, his eyes like chips of agate. "Not a damned thing, outlander. You're on your own."

IT HAD BEEN SNOWING overnight, and a thin carpet of powdery white lay across the hunting trail northward. In the first half hour or so they crossed tracks with a number of animals—a small herd of deer, a buck and half a dozen does, was J.B.'s assessment. Overlaying them was the pad marks of a hunting cougar.

Michael was perched uncomfortably aboard a rawboned one-eyed burro that lurched along with an awkward sideways gait. After less than ten minutes he was starting to moan, shifting in the saddle, complaining that his ass was hurting.

"It'll likely blister. Then they burst. Then you get new ones. Each time it hardens you up a little." J.B. laughed. "Give it a couple of months and you'll start enjoying it, lad."

"Because I'm a man of peace, John Dix, I will not wish you roasting in hell for that. But I wish you an eternity on the back of this cross-grained, vile creature."

The Armorer had a small bay mare, and Doc rode a ferocious-looking stallion, as black as midnight. But he was delighted to discover, in spite of its menacing appearance, that it was actually a calm and gentle mount.

Ryan had never been the best of horsemen, but he found the ambling skewbald was surefooted and biddable, picking its way through the icy rutted mud with hardly a slip.

There wasn't much conversation between the four men. The talking and the arguments had all taken place around the middle of the night. After that it had simply been a matter of getting on with the first part of the job—traveling the eighty miles or so to Yuma and finding if the killers were there, pick them up and take them safely back to Vista and the gentle vengeance of the giant baron, Alferd Nelson.

"We know anything about patrols from Yuma?" J.B. asked, heeling his mount alongside Ryan at a stretch where the trail had widened.

"No. Coburn was scathing about the way Sidler runs the ville. Says that there aren't sec men. Not like at Vista."

"Just the bullies and the deviants with the blasters," J.B. said contemptuously.

"Sounds that way."

"Could there be hunters?" Michael asked from just behind them. "Like those three men we saw shot?"

Ryan nodded, shrugging his shoulders against the cold easterly wind. "Could be, Michael. Closer we get, the more careful we have to be."

"Hellfire and bloody perdition!"

"What's up, Doc?" Ryan turned around in the

saddle, easing the muscles in his thighs by standing in the stirrups.

"If the Good Lord had intended us to ride horses, he would have provided us with better padding across our backsides."

"Can we stop for a break?" the teenager asked. "I've got to answer Nature's call."

"Got miles to go today," Ryan warned. "Ten days there and back. Going to use up four of those in plain traveling. Coburn says the trail's easy in summer. Not so easy with snow."

Michael swung from the saddle, looking for somewhere to tether the burro.

"Tie it properly. Don't just loop the bridle over a snagged branch," J.B. told him. "Lose an animal and we're in triple-deep shit."

The teenager nodded, sighing to himself. "I'm not stupid, you know. The way you and Ryan treat me, it's like you think I can't be trusted."

Ryan watched him, his hands folded on the pommel of his saddle. "Not trust in the way you mean it. You wouldn't have gone a single hour with us if we thought you couldn't be trusted, Michael."

He was unzipped, the amber stream of urine steaming as it splashed against the bole of a piñon pine. "So what do you mean by trust, Ryan?"

"We warn you about not doing something stupe,

then probably you won't do it. Odds are you wouldn't have done it anyway. But—and it's a big 'but,' that carries all our lives with it—you *might* do something foolish. No point in us saying that you shouldn't have done it. Not afterward. Too late then.''

Michael climbed onto the back of his mount, wincing as he lowered himself onto the saddle. "Only stupid thing is starting on this trip. We could've run for it. All of us."

Doc blew his nose on his swallow's-eye kerchief. "Man who runs today is only too likely to run for all of his life. Die on your feet, rather than struggle to live on your knees, my boy."

Michael didn't answer him. He kicked his booted heels into the flanks of the burro, pushing it on toward the north.

IT WAS a largely uneventful day. During the morning there was a sudden rise in the temperature, and it rained heavily. Driving gray clouds raced in from the east, shredding themselves on the jagged peaks all around.

The snow turned to slush, pouring off the paths, carrying red dirt with it. A small stream at their left became swollen into a frothing torrent, almost within minutes.

Around noon, with fog pressing down into the

valleys, it became colder once more. The rain turned to sleet, then to a brief flurry of fresh snow. The water and mud froze again, making the footing treacherous for the animals.

Within the hour they all reined in, responding to an ear-filling, thunderous roar from the far side of the valley, somewhere up ahead.

"Avalanche," Ryan said. "Changes in the weather often triggers them."

"Look." Michael stood up, pointing to the left, about five miles to the north.

A huge cloud of powdery white snow was funneling into the air, like the turbulent remnants of a vast nuke explosion.

"Seen them move faster than a wag on full throttle," J.B. commented.

Doc wiped his face with his sleeve. "Could we break for a small snack, do you think, my dear Ryan? If it's not too much trouble. I disremember when I've felt so jolted and jarred."

Ryan guessed that they'd covered around thirty miles since they left the ville of Vista. Not the fastest progress in the world, but not too bad, considering the weather and the state of the trails. It would bring them into Yuma during daylight tomorrow.

"Sure," he said. "We'll take fifteen. Then we push on."

J.B. SEEMED UNUSUALLY QUIET.

Ryan had ridden the length and breadth of Deathlands with him and knew well enough that something was very wrong.

Doc and Michael had walked over to watch the stream as it rolled down the valley, stretching their legs and trying to ease some of the stiffness from the joints.

The skewbald snickered as it heard something moving in the undergrowth. Both Ryan and J.B. went for their blasters, relaxing as a stout beaver waddled unconcernedly across the trail, its tail plowing a furrow through the fresh snow.

Ryan laughed, but J.B. simply stared at the plump, glistening animal, watching it as it plopped into the water.

"What is it?"

The Armorer turned and looked at Ryan. "That easy to tell?"

"Yeah. For me. Probably not for the others."

"Krysty?"

"Said last night she had a feeling of something troubling you. Something that she figured wasn't that good."

J.B. packed away the rest of his beef jerky in his saddlebag. "I don't think I want to talk about it, Ryan."

"Fair enough. Have to ask if it's going to affect

what we're doing, where we're going. Something ahead in Yuma?''

"It might be." J.B. took off his glasses and polished them on a strip of white cotton rag from one of his capacious pockets.

Ryan leaned forward. "Come on. This isn't some fucking game!"

"Dark night, Ryan! Think I don't know that? Course I do. But—"

"But what, J.B.?"

Doc and Michael had looked around, hearing the raised voices.

"But I don't know, Ryan. All right? When I know, then you'll know. Something I'm not sure of. Something about Yuma. When I know, then you'll know it as well. All right?"

"Have to be." Ryan stood. "Come on. Let's hit the trail again."

THE SNOW FLURRIES ceased in the middle of the afternoon. The wind dropped and so did the temperature, bringing a biting, dry cold.

The sun was already out of sight beyond the western white-tops, immersing the valleys in gloomy shadows when Ryan decided that they'd best look for a campsite for the night. As far as he could make out from Coburn's map, they'd ridden more than fifty miles in the day, and were now getting into the sort of region where Sidler just might have scouting parties out, watching the roads from the south.

Though, if Nelson hadn't made any move toward revenge for his son's murder in all those months, Sidler probably figured the baron was going to let it lie.

There'd been a small avalanche from high up the stark slopes to their right. It had been enough to bring down some of the smaller pines, tumbling them one against the other, blocking the trail.

They all dismounted, Michael with a bitten-off cry of real pain from the chafing of the saddle.

Ryan led the way, walking his horse around the fallen trees, aware of the brooding stillness of the forest at evening—a stillness that was suddenly broken by a woman's cry from around the bend of the trail, not far ahead of them.

"You double-damned and bloody dog! Take one step nearer to me and I will slit my throat open from ear to ear!"

Ryan dropped the bridle, drew the SIG-Sauer and started to run forward.

Chapter Eighteen

"I will see your bastard child dead at my feet before I leave this church, madam! Mine oath upon a limpet's walking staff!"

"And I with it, base villain."

Ryan burst through the fringe of stunted spruce trees, snow dusting his head and shoulders, his blaster gripped in his right hand.

The three people in the clearing all turned at his entrance, their mouths gaping, eyes wide with terror.

A stout man, red-cheeked, and wearing a long cloak in shocking vermilion and thigh-length boots in ragged black suede held a huge cutlass, obviously made from plywood, and painted silver.

He was threatening the kneeling woman with it. She was slightly built, with light blond hair and a pale complexion. Her dress was mud-stained around the hem and was a deep rich green, decorated at the throat with scalloped silver embroidery.

Standing by a horse-drawn wag was a lean

young man with a crooked back, and a livid red scar on his face tugging down the left eye. He was holding a sheaf of tattered paper.

The side of the wagon was covered in a weather-soiled tarpaulin, but Ryan didn't have time to try to read the faded words painted across it.

He skidded to a halt, aware of J.B., Michael and Doc rushing through the trees behind him.

The man with the sword held it before him in a dramatic and utterly futile gesture of defence. "We are but poor traveling folks, but I do swear that I will sell mine honor as dear as any prince in Christendom!"

"Put the wooden blade down," Ryan said, holstering the SIG-Sauer.

"What's going on?" J.B. was at Ryan's shoulder, the Uzi ready for action. "Heard the shouting and followed you."

Now there was a moment to decipher the lettering on the canvas side of the wagon—Monsignor Capestrano, Madame Morte and Supporting Company. Classics Old and New in the Finest Dramatic Fashion.

"They are journeying thespians," Doc panted, arriving a poor fourth.

"What?" Ryan turned around to look at the old man. "You mean actors?"

The woman was on her feet, brushing her dress

with nervous, birdlike gestures, a faltering smile pasted onto the white face. "Indeed, gentlemen, we are of that acting profession. You caught us in rehearsal for the suicide scene in *Lucia of Lisbon,* a famous old tragedy of incest and mistaken identity."

"Sorry to have frightened you," Ryan said. "Heard the threats and—"

"Came running to defend the honor of a soiled virgin," the man concluded, dropping his lath cutlass and striding forward with hand outstretched. "And that does you the very greatest of honor, sir, upon my soul it does."

"You never met Doc Tanner, here, did you?" J.B. asked, struck by the similarity in the weird way of speaking.

"No, I have not yet had that pleasure. But I must introduce us to you. I am—" he turned to the wagon with a sweeping gesture "—I am that Monsignor Diego Capestrano, proprietor of this company. The lady is Madame Ellie Morte, diva and diseuse extraordinaire, who has performed before some of the greatest barons in all Deathlands."

"Who's he?" Ryan asked, pointing to the dark-clothed young man.

"Knuckles," Capestrano replied shortly. "He is stage manager, prompter, horse wrangler, keeper of the finances and player of small parts, various."

"I'm Ryan Cawdor. This is J. B. Dix, Doc Tanner and Michael Brother."

There was a general shaking of hands.

Ellie Morte seemed to Ryan to linger a little over his grip, and he felt her index finger brush the inside of his palm. Close up, he saw that she was older than he'd at first guessed, her face layered in powder and makeup. He also noticed that she was trembling, though that could easily have come from the shock of his bursting out of the trees with his blaster in his hand.

Knuckles retreated to his position by the wagon as soon as he'd offered a cursory hand to the four newcomers, where he studied the script of *Lucia of Lisbon*.

"Shy," Capestrano explained. "Many actors suffer in a similar way." He looked around the clearing. "Can we offer you a share in our humble repast? There is some venison pies and a decent portion of yesterday's bread."

"Day before yesterday," Knuckles corrected, managing a shy grin.

"And some ale from our last venue," the lady offered.

"Where are you going?" Doc asked.

"To a place called Yuma. A half day north of here." Capestrano looked at Ryan. "Do you know anything of it, sir?"

"Yes. A little." He rubbed his hands together, the germ of an idea beginning to take a faltering shape in his mind. "But first we'll bring our horses here and tether them. We've got some beef jerky that we can share with you, and some bread that was baked this very morning."

IT WAS a pleasant and entertaining evening, with a small, bright fire and sufficient food to layer the stomach.

Ryan surmised that they were far enough from the enemy's ville to be safe from any random patrols. In any case the surrounding forest was so thick that their camp fire would be visible only from a hundred paces or less.

He had described himself and the others as simply traveling workers, hinting that they'd once been sec men but that there'd been trouble in the past, giving the impression of hired shootists, without actually saying so.

But his part of the conversation was mainly limited to listening.

Monsignor Diego Capestrano not only kept up his end of the talk, he managed to keep up everyone else's as well.

One moment he was the stammering baron of a ville in the Glades asking them to do a recitation of his own poetry. Next he was playing a part from an ancient play, someone who was going to have his heart cut out for a debt to a vengeful woman. Or the baron whose powerful friends had turned against him and all assassinated him.

Ellie Morte was quieter, but as the ale flowed from a small keg in the bed of the wagon, she brightened.

Doc was totally fascinated with the small group of strolling players, plying them with questions about their repertoire.

Capestrano struck a pose in front of the fire, the light flickering off his rotund cheeks. His voice was rich and round, sounding as though it had been matured in a cask of fine old brandy.

"I play all leading gentlemen, merry or sad or wealthy or poor. Those who have lent money at scurrilous interest or have returned after a grievous shipwreck to claim their inheritance. Sadly we have lost several members of our poor company and are much reduced in what we can perform. I still do my very best to bring culture to frontier pestholes. I essay most of Shakespeare's heroes— Macbeth and Richard Two and Three. Henry Four in both parts, as well as Five and Six. And Hamlet, the saddest prince of all."

"Or to take arms against a sea of troubles," Doc said, pausing melodramatically. "And by opposing, end them."

Ellie Morte clapped her hands. "Wonderfully spoken, Dr. Tanner. And you are versed in the classics. So rare!"

"Doc's done some acting," Ryan said, the plan instantly crystallizing. "In fact all of us have done a bit in our times."

J.B. was quickest, glancing over at Ryan, then looking into the fire. Doc shook his head modestly, but didn't argue. Ryan had remembered that the old man had sometimes spoken about appearing with amateur companies in his youth.

Michael was slower. "Acting, Ryan?"

"At Nil-Vanity. You said you'd been on the stage there." Ryan tried to catch his eye to warn him not to argue.

"I didn't... You've got me mixed up with somebody else, Ryan."

Loss-cutting time. "That's odd. Sure it was you." Ryan shook his head, pleasantly puzzled. Inwardly he was furious that the teenager's stupidity had jeopardized his scheme for getting into Yuma without any awkward questions.

Belatedly Michael realized the subtext of what was going on and clapped his hand to his head. "Oh, I get it! I said that I always *wanted* to do some acting. But I never had the chance."

Better late than never. "Sure, that must've been it."

Capestrano and the woman exchanged glances.

"As I said, our little company is, unfortunately, depleted. It would assist us enormously if Michael and the worthy Dr. Tanner might join us. Just for a few performances," Capestrano added hastily. "Nothing too difficult or demanding. If there were to be any profits, then it might be possible for a small share to come your way."

Ryan nodded. So far, so good.

Chapter Nineteen

Ryan was awakened by the feeling of movement close by, in the blackness of the deep forest night.

The fire had died down to a cupful of gray ash. He could just make out a patch of star-spangled sky through the branches of the spruces above him. But the light of the moon didn't penetrate down to the snow-dusted earth.

His hand was around the butt of the SIG-Sauer P-226 before he even realized he was awake.

Ryan's night vision in his one eye was excellent, and he could see the dim shape of someone, crouching between him and the large rear wheels of the actors' wagon.

"Ellie?" he whispered.

"Yeah. Hope I didn't make you jump. Couldn't sleep."

Ryan sat up, still holding the blaster. He had lived into his late thirties by doing everything he could not to get careless. Just because a frail-looking woman came to you in the night, it didn't mean she wasn't holding a needle-thin dagger to thrust between your vertebrae.

The cemeteries of Deathlands were filled with men, and a few women, who'd grievously overestimated their own invulnerability.

Ellie had shuffled a little closer to him. "Can I come under your blanket, Ryan?" the woman whispered.

"Why?"

Now she was almost close enough to touch. In the stillness, Ryan could catch the scent of her body, see the pale blur of her face and the tumbled whiteness of her hair.

"Couldn't sleep. Capestrano snores like a hog in muck."

"Where's Knuckles?"

"Under the wag. Always sleeps there. Seems happy enough."

"What is it, Ryan?" The quiet, familiar voice of J.B. came from the shadows.

"Nothing, J.B., nothing. You can go back to sleep again."

"Sure." The man's breathing instantly grew steady as the Armorer dozed once more.

"Can I, Ryan?"

He hesitated. Ellie wasn't unattractive, but Ryan had never been a man on the alert for the offer of an easy lay.

"I don't think so."

She was close enough to touch him, her hand resting on his thigh beneath the blanket.

"You got a wife?"

"Sort of."

"She wouldn't know if you had some funning with me, Ryan."

"I'd know."

"Nobody else."

"How about Capestrano?"

"What about him?"

Her hand had reached the top of his thigh, and Ryan could feel the unrestrainable beginnings of arousal. "No," he said, stopping her.

"Capestrano and me have an understanding. We've known each other for years. Mebbe too many years. He drinks some. Not that interested in making the beast with two backs. Can't raise much more than a smile these days, Ryan."

"Answer is still that I don't think so."

"You want to get into Yuma, pretend to be part of our troupe, Ryan."

Despite her frail appearance, Ellie Morte had layers of steel.

Ryan saw no point in lying to her. She obviously knew anyway. "Yeah."

"Why?"

Her hand was back on his leg, and he allowed it to remain. For a while.

"There's a murdered child. Slaughtered. Men who did it could be in Yuma. That's all there is to it, Ellie."

"I see." Now she could feel him reacting to her, and she laughed. "You want to, don't you, Ryan? We both know it."

"Wanting something doesn't make it right, Ellie. We both know that, too."

"Yeah." Her fingers relaxed their hold on him for a moment.

"You tell me that you'll ask Capestrano to turn us away if I don't fuck you, and I'll have to fuck you, Ellie. That what you want?"

She leaned over and kissed him on the lips, the tip of her tongue probing between his teeth. Ryan tasted her excitement. And something else. Something was not quite right. For a moment he couldn't recognize it. A touch of...what was it?

Decay.

Ellie Morte was seriously ill.

He wondered about the dreadful rad scar that adorned the cheek of Knuckles.

She was moving, straightening to stand above him. His eye had adjusted to the filtered moonlight, and he could see that Ellie was smiling.

"All right, Ryan," she whispered. "I won't rock

the boat for you. Tomorrow we'll be in Yuma. All of us.''

"That's good," he said. "Thanks."

She poked him with her toe. "Bastard." Then she was gone, padding silently back to her bed in the wagon.

Chapter Twenty

Despite his objections, Dean had been ordered to sleep in the same bedroom as Krysty and Mildred. He'd argued so bitterly that, eventually, his father had taken him to one side, kneeling and putting his mouth close to the boy's ear. "Could tell you that I need a man to watch over the two women, but you're not a stupe. Truth is, I want you all to stay together. Watch over one another. All three of you. You understand me?"

The boy had agreed.

Mildred and Krysty had agreed that they'd stay together with the boy as much as possible. Even if it meant offending the baron. Ryan's last words had been to warn them what to do if the ten days were up and he hadn't returned with the prisoners.

"I don't think that Nelson's the sort of man who would break his word. Won't jump the gun until the ten days are up. But that doesn't mean you aren't triple-red careful."

The first evening they'd asked to have food served to them in their room.

Rick Coburn escorted the serving woman who pushed the squeaking trolley carrying the supper, taking the lids off the dishes with all the panache of a traveling magician.

"Leek soup with cress. Trout, poached in chicken juices. A sort of messy thing with peas and sweet potatoes. Some meat. What kind's that? Pork? Or is it mutton?"

"Pork, with apple sauce," the servant replied with a muddled curtsy.

"Right. And there's some okra and some carrots. Baron's not that interested in pudding stuff, but that's a cherry-and-pear pie with some cream. Ale or apple juice to drink."

Krysty looked over the spread. "It's good. Thanks for it."

"Welcome, Krysty." He shooed the woman out ahead of him, pausing in the doorway. "After you've finished, I'll collect Dean and show him a wolf one of our patrols caught and brought in."

Mildred paused, with a ladle of soup in midair. "Why's that?"

Coburn shrugged. "Not mine to ask. I'm just the guy does what he's told. Baron says to jump, I just say 'How high?' That's me."

The black woman advanced on him, waving the heavy spoon. "Don't play the dumb-ass, red-neck peckerwood with us, Coburn! Why does Nelson want the boy away from us?''

"So's he can speak to you two in private. That's why."

"What's he want to say, Coburn?" Krysty asked, glancing around to see that Dean was already devouring the fish and sweet potatoes, paying no attention to anyone else.

"Told you. I wasn't raised to ask stupe questions of seven-foot-tall barons. Ask him yourself after the meal."

THE SEC BOSS KEPT his promise, collecting Dean after the boy had finished his third gut-stuffing portion of the fruit pie.

"Real big wolf, son. Got a bullet in a foreleg, but it's still damned lively. Ripped the belly out of one of the horses when the patrol tried to get it netted."

"Coburn..." Krysty said, not quite sure how to go on.

His eyes were glittering slits of midnight jet, his mouth a steel trap. "Listen, I've told you. Far as he goes, you can trust Baron Alferd Nelson. And you can trust me all the way to the wire. You don't believe that, well..." He shrugged, and left the room with his arm around the skinny boy.

The woman came scuttling in to clear away the

dirty plates and dishes, resisting the efforts of Mildred and Krysty to get her talking.

"Told to keep my flapper shut" was all she kept repeating.

Less than five minutes later there was a gentle rapping on the paneled oak door.

"Come in, Baron," Krysty called. "Doors in this ville keep us in. Won't keep you out."

The gigantic man seemed even bigger, ducking under the vaulted ceiling. He was holding a dark green bottle, its top wrapped in golden foil, and three tall, narrow glasses in cut crystal. In his enormous hands they looked like something from a doll's house.

"Can I offer you something from my cellars? Something quite wonderful?"

"What?" Krysty asked.

"This." He held up the bottle. "You will never have tasted anything like this before."

Mildred peered at the faded label. "It's a 1982 Moët & Chandon. Fine imperial, extra-dry champagne. I'll drink to that, Baron. Long as it's been kept properly it could be fair."

"Fair!"

"Let's break it open, and see if it's good as I remember it."

"The skills have vanished that went to make this nectar, woman."

"Typical. Bad-mouth the living and speak well of the dead."

Nelson shook his head, the electric lamps on the walls bouncing light off his mane of silvery hair and the long white beard.

"I've never met anyone like you two ladies."

"Ladies?" Krysty repeated, smiling. "Moment ago we were just plain old women, Baron."

"Shall I open this champagne?" he asked, looking around the room for somewhere to put the glasses before setting them on a small round table, inlaid with a pattern of onyx chips.

"You got Dean out of the way. Speak your mind, Baron," Krysty said.

"Give us a piece of your mind, Baron," Mildred added. "Give us peace of mind."

"I don't understand," he said, wrestling with the wire knotted around the top of the old bottle.

Mildred laughed. "A piece of ass don't give you peace of mind, Baron."

The cork erupted from the bottle with a satisfying explosion, bouncing off the ceiling and landing in a round wooden bowl.

"There!" he exclaimed, as though he were grateful not to have to persevere with the conversation with the two bizarre outland women.

The pale, straw-colored liquid frothed into the glasses.

"Before we drink, Baron Nelson," Krysty said, "tell us what you want." She held up her hand. "No. Tell us now. Quick and simple."

"Very well. I am a lonely man. My son Zebe was my heart, my life. Clare, the slut, gave me only the one child. But he was worth the rest of the world. Now he is in his grave and I am alone once more. No child. No wife."

"We know all this," Mildred said quietly, touched by the man's massive grief.

"I do not know other women. Whores and servants. A wife or two of my sec men. Unworthy."

Krysty nodded. "And you think that me and Mildred might be worthy?"

Nelson was holding one of the glasses up to the light, staring at the myriad tiny bubbles that were ascending the misted crystal.

"If Cawdor brings me my righteous vengeance, I shall keep my word and let all of you go. But if he does not..."

"You father more children on us, and you also have the bonus of an instant son. Dean." Krysty shook her head. "You got the size and the fortress and some good sec men. But that won't be enough. Not by a country mile, Baron."

"You're threatening me, Krysty Wroth? That isn't a wise move."

"Like Ryan says... Well, he says it's a man

called Trader used to say this. You got to realize that there's a serious difference between making a threat and giving a promise. That wasn't a threat, Baron, as you know. It was a promise."

Her bright red hair was coiled protectively around her skull, like a cap of living fire. Her emerald eyes gleamed at him like a cornered cobra.

Nelson nodded slowly, his hand on the tasseled hilt of the long saber. "Think I could come to believe that."

"And live to regret it," Mildred added. "You'd never be able to turn your back as long as any of us still lived."

"Even little Dean?"

"Little Dean's seen more death than you, Baron. I'd stake my life on that. He might only be ten... no, turned eleven now. But he's sent grown men off to buy the farm."

"All right, ladies. There's nine days still to go. Now a truce. Try this champagne. A rarity."

It was tainted. Sour and bitter, with the flavor of sickness and decay. Undrinkable.

Chapter Twenty-One

Knuckles drove the wagon up the winding black-top into Yuma. They'd picked their way out of the surrounding forest, finding that the maze of tracks all eventually uncoiled into a single highway, past the ruins of derelict gas stations, gift stores and fast-food restaurants.

The blacktop started to level off, but it was narrow, a sheer cliff of snow-smeared granite rising to their right and a steep drop of a thousand feet to a shadowed valley.

Across to their left they could see several rows of rusted and tumbled metal pylons, with the remains of corroded cable snaking between them. Michael pointed to it, asking what it could be.

Capestrano answered the teenager. "Back around the end of the last century, people took vacations in Colorado. They paid huge amounts of jack to strap on skis and fall down the mountains. Those were sky wags that took them up to the tops so they could fall down again so that they could ride up and fall down again. You get the picture, son?"

"Yeah. I've heard of it."

Doc rubbed his hands together against the cold. "Yuma was one of the custom-built resorts in these parts. Places like Vail and Aspen and Crested Butte. I think the word was *trendy,* to describe them in those days."

"Thought we'd have met some others on the road," J.B. said. "Day's well on."

Knuckles laughed, a hoarse, grating sound that made the five animals prick up their ears. "You never been to no pesthole like Yuma. Nobody gets up much before noon."

"This is the only way in and out?" Ryan asked. "No backtrack?"

Capestrano shook his head. He'd climbed into the wag again, to sit alongside Knuckles. "No. Believe not."

J.B. had been appraising the approach to the ville with the eyes of a combat veteran. "Reckon that Nelson was right," he said quietly to Ryan. "Need a couple of wags, and even then you could take some serious losses."

"Yeah. Easy site to hold. Difficult one to try to capture."

Now they had reached a leveling-out point, and were able to see that many of the buildings were multifloored condominium blocks. And they were also able to see the first of the sec barriers, a row of rusting oil drums, probably filled with concrete, Ryan guessed, strung across the road. There was a gap in the middle, wide enough for a single wag to get through, but a red-and-white-striped metal pole had been placed across the space. Four or five men lounged in a ramshackle hut at the side of the blacktop.

"Think that the killers are going to be out and open around the ville?" J.B. asked as he rode alongside Ryan.

"Don't know. By now they'll likely think they've got a fresh ace from the murder. Won't be looking for a revenge party now."

"Oh, yeah." The Armorer brushed a hand over his forehead, edging back the fedora. "It seem hot to you, Ryan?"

"Fireblast, no! Turn a man's balls to beaten brass, this cold."

"I feel hot. Sort of sick and dizzy."

"Rein in a moment."

Knuckles drew the tired horse to a halt, looking back to see what was wrong.

"J.B.'s feeling ill."

"Let him ride in the wagon with me," Ellie suggested, appearing from the back of the rig. She wore a thermal two-piece in black leather, with a hood lined in red satin.

"Yeah, think I will."

Ryan looked at his old friend, knowing that something was going on, but not having the least idea what it might be. J. B. Dix wasn't the sort of person who gave in to a sudden illness, and he certainly didn't look sick.

"I'll lead your horse," he said.

"Thanks." The Armorer slipped from the saddle, taking the Smith & Wesson and the Uzi.

"J.B.?" Ryan hesitated.

"What?"

"You know."

A ghost of a smile flitted across J.B.'s face, his eyes invisible behind the flat, dull lenses of his glasses. "Mebbe. You and me, Ryan..."

"What?"

"Been together way too long. Know each other better than a man and woman been married fifty years."

"So, what is it? Why do you want to hide out in the wag?"

"Reasons."

"Like you said before? So, on a need-to-tell basis, that it?"

"That's it." He handed Ryan the bridle of the little mare and climbed into the wag, helped by

Ellie. Knuckles clicked his tongue at the horse, and they rolled toward the checkpoint.

RYAN MOTIONED for Doc and Michael to keep toward the rear of the wag, not wanting to draw too much attention to them.

Only one of the sec men bothered to stroll over to examine the newcomers. He was skinny and unshaved, carrying what might once have been an AK-47. But it was so battered and covered in dirt and grease that it was almost impossible to guess. He was wearing a torn camouflage jacket and dark blue pants. A silver lightning flash dangled askew from one ragged lapel and seemed to be the only nod toward any sort of uniform.

"Who are you?" he asked.

Capestrano pointed to the painted sign on the canvas side of the wag. "You may see for yourself, my good man."

"Don't read, shithead."

"For which welcome, much thanks."

"What?" The muzzle of the AK-47 moved toward Capestrano's rubicund face.

"Nothing. We are actors, such stuff as dreams are made of, and we have come here to the ville of Yuma to perform some snatches from the great dramas. May we enter?"

"Let them in!" one of the other guards shouted. "They got sluts with them?"

"No. We have Madame Ellie Morte, tragedian and chanteuse, who has performed before many of the great barons of Deathlands."

"She suck cocks?" a third sec man asked, pulling himself upright, scratching at his crotch as he walked toward the wag.

Ellie stuck her head through the front flap of the rig. "Only if they belong to men, so you have no need to worry," she called, and was rewarded by a bellow of raucous laughter from the other guards.

"She got your measure, inch-dick," yelled the one with the AK-47.

"Them on horses with you?" asked a tall man with a long salt-and-pepper beard.

"A poor part of our small company. May we pass on through, friend?"

"I ain't your fuckin' friend, you ponced up little cornholer."

"Let them through, Wilt," the one with the beard ordered.

"Guess so. Might have to meet up with Wizard Sidler. He's the man around Yuma."

"Of course. Recommend any good place to stay? Light on roaches and heavy on food and drink?"

"And clean on beds," Ellie insisted. "With a

room big enough for us to put on a show? Anywhere fit that bill?''

"You can *lay* a show on for me anytime, lady,'' stated the sec man she'd put down a few moments earlier. "How about that?''

"I reckon I could find a use for you, mister. How would it be if I sat on your face, and you got to keep that big mouth of yours open for me?''

He sniggered, face red with excitement, tongue licking his thick lips. "I'd like that a lot. Any fuckin' time.''

Ellie nodded briskly. "Fine. Reckon you'll be better than any outhouse.''

"Why, she gutshot you all over again, Harve,'' called the man with the blaster over the wave of embarrassed laughter, carrying that note of everyone thanking their gods that it hadn't been them trying to take on the pale woman.

"That's not fuckin' funny.'' Harve turned his back and walked away.

"Yeah. Best place is the Snow Palace. Up three blocks. Make a left. Can't miss it. Got its own livery stable as well.''

Capestrano stood and bowed. "I'm much obliged to you. If you want, I'm happy to offer you and your stout comrades freebies for the first show tomorrow night. Just come and ask.''

The barrier was lifted and the augmented Monsignor Diego Capestrano theater company was waved on through into the ville of Yuma.

Chapter Twenty-Two

From the 2000 edition of the *Mobil Travel Guide to the Southwest and South Central,* the section on Colorado:

Yuma. Founded 1893. Population 1794. Elevation 9125 ft. Area Code 303.

This picturesque old mining town had been turned in the last ten years into one of the finest and most exclusive centers of the winter resort business. Its rowdy silver-mining days are long behind it, but much of its late-Victorian architecture has been retained, including the Civil Hall, where such luminaries as Oscar Wilde and Charles Dickens came to perform while touring the country.

There are four triple and six double chair lifts with two surface lifts. Rentals, schools, snowmaking, nursery, 97 runs, the longest 2.4 miles. Vertical drop 2,450 ft. Also 21.3 miles of groomed cross-country trails and in excess of 150 miles of wilderness trails with sleigh rides and snowmobiles.

Yuma boasts the largest number of rented apartments on the Colorado Plateau, available for short or long lets. Prices range from moderate (few) up to luxury.

The guide went on to list the hotels, motels, inns, motor hotels and resorts, including the Victorian Imperial Hotel, once frequented by members of the czar's family, and the picturesquely named Best Western Snow Crystal.

Restaurants included all manner of ethnic eateries—Thai, Malayan, Szechuan, Mandarin, Italian, Spanish, German, Serbian, Herzogovinian and Flemish.

Yuma's regular attractions had the usual tours of historic houses, in a horse-drawn brougham, as well as a Heritage Gallery and Mining Museum, with active dioramas. The Fin'n'Tail fish hatchery, in the valley below the town, was well stocked with cutthroat and rainbow trout.

The Mobil Guide finished up its entry:

Yuma has replaced the older resorts such as Vail and Aspen, and is now *the* center for those who want to relax and enjoy themselves without worrying too much about the nickels and dimes. Comfort and quality in the finest surroundings.

THAT WAS THEN. And this is now.

Every now and again in Deathlands you might come across a cheaply and badly printed little booklet called *Frontier Pestholes of the Southwest*. It was a guide to some of the villes that dotted the region. Many of them were like the small mining communities of the late nineteenth century that boomed and busted, sometimes in a single year. Like most guidebooks, this one was instantly out of date, but the reference to Yuma had some interest.

Once the resort of the rich and famous, this is a bottom-of-the-barrel pesthole. The ruins of ski lifts makes the hills around dangerous, and there is only one road in and one road out of the place and that's guarded in a sort of way.

Baron last time I was there was called Wizard Sidler, and he runs a sloppy ship up there. Sec men are lazy and likely to blast anyone they don't much like the look of, so step careful and have a handful of loose jack to pay them off if you have to. Sidler's fortress in Yuma is in the ruins of a cinema complex where he watches a collection of old vids. Interesting if you like that sort of thing, which I don't but you might. There are a few gaudies and scabby sluts who pox you just by breathing on you.

Conclusion. Give Yuma a big miss if you don't want to finish up getting hit.

This is now.

Chapter Twenty-Three

The Snow Palace wasn't the dirtiest flophouse that Ryan had ever stayed in. There'd been one in the Glades that flooded every time the tide turned.

Knuckles drove the rig around the back of the three-floor frame building and into the livery stable, where a limping old woman took in their horses and directed them along a side alley to the entrance of the self-styled hotel.

They took three rooms on the top story. Capestrano had one with a balcony overlooking the ville's main drag. Ellie had a smaller room at the side, while Ryan and the other three took a large suite with a broken window that looked out over the snowy mountains to the north of the ville.

Knuckles chose to sleep in the loft of the livery stable.

The woman who registered them, Rosie Owen, was in her late thirties and wore a greasy dress that looked like it had first seen duty in the camp kitchens at Shiloh.

"Want to eat down here or in your rooms?" she

asked, wiping the back of her hand across her dribbling nose. "Costs more if I have to bring it all the way up to you."

"You do the cooking?" Ellie asked.

"Sure."

"In my room."

"Rest of you?"

"Downstairs," Ryan replied.

"In the room," J.B. said simultaneously. His fedora was pulled down over his eyes, and he had looped a woolen scarf over his mouth and nose, hiding most of his face.

"You some kind of desperado waiting for a payroll?" the woman asked.

"No. Got a cold."

"We'll all eat in our rooms," Ryan said. "What time'll it be?"

"When I've gotten it all ready, mister." She bit her lip, a pudgy hand burrowing under the dress, somewhere in the vicinity of her sagging breasts. "Damn this!"

"What ails you, madam?" Doc inquired.

"Got me an ulcer on my tit. Ate up most of one nipple. Keeps leaking blood and yellow stuff all over me."

Capestrano put a hand across his rosebud mouth, his normally rosy complexion turning pale. "I fear that my appetite has suddenly abandoned me."

Mrs. Owen told them that all newcomers had to report to Wizard Sidler's headquarters. "Old flick-house down the street. Baron'll be there. Don't go out much these days."

The others went up the dusty stairs toward their rooms, but Ryan stayed behind.

"Something I can do for you, dearie?" Rosie asked. "Reasonable prices. Won't get diseased like you would with most of the gaudies."

"Mebbe later. Heard there might be a few men I know from way back. Came here months ago. Probably in with the baron."

"They come and go," she said. "You got any names for them?"

"Could be six men. One called Jennison. Another was Grant. One was known as Julio, last time I met up with him."

"Oh, sure. Not six men. Five men and a woman. Part Indian. Name's Reena Miller." She laughed. "You got some very triple-wicked friends. Those five got a mean name around Yuma." The laugh grew louder, followed by a choking fit that brought tears into the woman's bloodshot eyes. "Oh, fuck me over sideways, dearie! Just that I thought how you had to be something special to get a name for mean around this ville."

"You said those five. You mean the five men? What about the woman?"

Rosie sniffed. "Reena's worse than the men. No, there's only five of them left now."

"What happened?"

Michael called from the stairs above. "You coming up, Ryan?"

"Yeah, in a minute. What happened to the other man?"

"Bob Maxwell. Fat bastard. Got his belly opened up with a shiv by a Mex trapper. Then Jennison blew him apart with a 12-gauge. Mex was dead before Bob even hit the floor."

"They hang out around Sidler's place?"

"Yeah." As Ryan turned toward the stairs, Rosie added, "Sure you wouldn't care for some real genuine cheap passion, dearie?"

Ryan didn't bother to reply.

When he reached their room, Ryan found Michael sitting at a table playing solitaire with a dog-eared pack of cards. Doc lay on the bed, eyes closed, chest rising and falling in a gentle rhythm.

J.B. stood by the window, flat against the wall, peering out through a tattered lace curtain. He was still wearing his fedora.

Ryan closed the door quietly behind him. "See anyone, J.B.?"

Doc blinked awake. "I agree with everything that the last speaker said," he muttered. "Wake me up when we finally reach the top of the eighth, there's a good fellow. Much obliged.'' Then he dropped off again.

The Armorer turned from the window. ''Nobody out there. So far, there doesn't seem much life in this ville. Been looking at those condo blocks. Most seem like they burned out years ago.''

''You see who you were looking for?'' There was an edge to Ryan's voice that made Michael glance up from his game.

''Red seven on black eight.'' J.B. sat on an old overstuffed sofa. ''All right. Could be someone here who knows me from the past.''

''Who?''

J.B. shook his head, taking off the hat and tossing it onto one of the other beds. ''Don't know. I don't know and I can't be sure. And I'm not going to talk about it, Ryan. Not unless I have to. And then I will. All right?''

''Sure. There's only five of our targets left. One got knifed in a fight. Five, including a woman called Reena Miller.''

''Who got chilled?''

''Fat guy called Bob Maxwell. He the one might know you?''

''No.'' J.B. shook his head. ''Only five left. And Nelson wants four back.''

''Or two if we also snatch Sidler.''

''Place seems carelessly run.'' J.B. walked

slowly around the room, hands clasped behind his back, passing Michael. "Black queen goes on red king," he said absently.

"Yeah. I figure we can get out of Yuma. But with prisoners it'll be slow going. Lose one, and we could lose the whole prize."

"We going to have to perform with Capestrano and his whore?"

"She wouldn't take kindly to being called that," Ryan told him. "What makes you think she'll put out? She make an offer you managed to refuse?"

J.B. sat on his bed, swinging up his legs. "As it happens... When we were coming through the checkpoint, she had my belt off and her hand around...inside my...before I stopped her."

"She tried me last night. Wanted to get inside my sleeping bag." He grinned at J.B.'s face, with its mix of emotions.

Michael laid the two of clubs on the three of diamonds. "There," he said. "Incidentally Ellie asked me to make love with her before she came over to you, Ryan. I told her I didn't think I wanted to. She didn't seem to mind too much."

RYAN WIPED THE KNIFE and spoon on his pants before risking putting them anywhere near his mouth. Capestrano and Ellie had joined them in the large room, where there was a table big enough to seat seven of them. Knuckles had limped in from the stables, eyes watering from the cold easterly wind blowing in over the Sawatch Range, reporting that the horses were all being well cared for.

To their amazement the food brought up by Rosie was appetizing, well-cooked and served in a range of dishes, ornamented with a blue-and-yellow dragon motif.

"Venison stew," she said, taking her thumb out of the tureen and sucking it. "Hung six weeks so it's rich and strong. There's refried beans with chilies I grew and dried myself. Soda bread and salted butter. And a dish of whipped potatoes there. Got some beer in the jugs." She picked something out from between her back teeth and flicked it across the room.

"Eat in good spirits," she said.

"THAT WAS EXCELLENT." Doc didn't quite manage to stifle a belch.

"Long as we don't all start to throw up around midnight." J.B. absently wiped the last of the gravy off his plate with the last of the bread. "It tasted fine. Just wish I could've stopped myself seeing that woman's filthy hands all over it."

Knuckles was looking at the tureen. "Anyone mind if I lick it out?"

Capestrano folded his hands over his stomach. "My dear boy, this is liberty hall. Eat away and right welcome."

Ellie dabbed at her mouth with the corner of a kerchief, embroidered with tiny strawberries. "That was good ale," she said. Her cheeks were unusually flushed. Ryan couldn't help noticing that her fingers trembled a little as she poured herself another mug of beer.

"What do we do now?" Michael asked. "We learn this play?"

Ryan pushed himself back from the table and stood, looking out over the mountains. By pressing his face to the cold glass he could just see along the backs of the houses on the street. It was growing dark, and he could make out flurries of snow, wreathing among the skeletal trees that lined the edge of the sheer precipice.

"Mebbe we should go see the baron, Wizard Sidler. Don't want sec men calling around to drag us to his place."

"Day two finished," J.B. warned.

"Yeah. Michael's right. If we're going to put on this play tomorrow night, we've got a shit lot of work to do."

Capestrano beamed. "Miss Morte and I will take the lion's share of the parts. Doc will be wonderful. I have him in mind for a shabby and irascible old man. Perhaps inebriated. The sort of fellow who runs around with a thick stick, compelling his nephew to marry an heiress."

Doc snatched up his lion's-head sword stick and flourished it. "Ah, the smell of the crowd and the roar of the greasepaint," he said, nearly knocking a small china figure of a ballerina off the table at his side with his cane.

"Simmer down, Doc." Ellie smiled. "Save it for tomorrow."

"I'll go check out the baron in the morning," Ryan said.

"I'll come with you," Michael offered.

"No. You must stay and learn your part for the performance," Capestrano insisted. "Perhaps John Dix will accompany you, Ryan?"

"No," said both J.B. and Ryan, the snapped word overlapping.

"Think I'd rather stay around here," the Armorer added. "Can't act, and this way I'll keep out of trouble. Mebbe use your room, Ellie, and watch over the ville."

"Of course."

The evening ended with everyone going to bed early. As Ryan lay there, the night sounds of Yuma occasionally disturbing him, he thought about J.B. He'd never seen his old friend so tense and edgy.

Outside there was an occasional burst of singing.

A couple of times a scream or a yell. Once a shot, away in the distance.

But Ryan eventually drifted into an uneasy sleep.

Chapter Twenty-Four

J.B. stood in the corridor, beckoning urgently to Ryan.

"What?"

The Armorer was wearing a small pair of glasses, with diamond-shaped, heavily smoked lenses. He held a slim-bladed knife in his right hand, using it to call Ryan toward him.

"What is it?"

J.B.'s mouth opened, but the only sound that Ryan heard was a faint buzzing, like a swarm of wasps, contained inside a tall chimney.

"No good, man," Ryan called. "I can't hear a plain word."

J.B. turned and started to walk away, shoulders slumped, as though he'd suffered some dreadful defeat. The passage extended into pools of deep shadow, with moonlit windows ranged along to the right. At irregular intervals there were sculpted heads on tall plinths of brown flecked marble.

As Ryan began to follow his oldest and closest friend through the sighing echoes of the empty house, he looked at each bust as he passed it, noticing that the nose had been hacked off each face, and that the eyes were savagely gouged pits of rough stone.

J.B.'s steel-cleated combat boots rang out as he moved down the corridor, but above the sound, Ryan could catch the susurration of a tinkling harpsichord, delicate, plangent notes.

"J.B.! Hold up there!"

As he stepped outside, the rain teemed down around him, soaking his hair and running behind the patch over his raw eye socket, the long barreled .38 revolver on his right hip banging painfully against his thigh as he ran through the dripping spruces.

J.B. had disappeared over the top of one of the large dunes, his foot marks barely visible in the powder-dry sand.

Ryan dug into his enormous reserves of strength, tackling the dusty path up the side of the cliff. Far below him he could see a white-necked condor, swinging across the valley on spread wings. The rock beneath his feet was crumbling, forcing him to go higher and higher.

"Come on, Ryan. Why don't you take the road less traveled?"

J.B.'s voice sounded oddly like Ryan's long-dead father, Baron Titus Cawdor, of the powerful ville of Front Royale.

Now the whole side of the mountain was sliding away. Each time Ryan jumped to a higher, parallel path, that too started to tumble. His boots scrabbled frantically for purchase.

"Secrets make for bad neighbors, Ryan."

"Wait for me, J.B., and I'll tell you what's happening."

The corridor was finished.

The row of sculpted heads was behind him, and all that remained in front of Ryan was a blank wall of dull sec steel.

He was vaguely aware of the sound of a war wag's engine, rumbling up a steep incline, struggling as though it were working at altitude. Coughing and spluttering, it seemed to be coming closer.

Ryan moved uneasily.

"Dark night!" J.B. sounded angry.

Ryan blinked his good eye, wincing at the brightness of the light that cut across the bedroom like an Apache lance.

"Stop snoring, Doc!"

This time it was Michael.

"Throw a pillow at the noisy old fart. Shut him up!"

Ryan finally woke up, feeling tired and ready for a few hours' more sleep.

THE BREAKFAST EGGS were over-easy. They were also over three weeks old and grievously over-cooked.

"We could use them to block off the big gap at the side of the window," Michael suggested. "Or shoot them at this Baron Sidler when we go after that gang."

Ryan had been sitting across the table from the teenager, with J.B. on his left and Doc picking thoughtfully at some green bacon on the right. Knuckles was checking out the horses while Capestrano and Ellie were having a working breakfast, discussing the play they were planning to put on that evening.

Ryan stood and walked toward Michael, who saw the expression on his face and got to his feet, adapting a defensive Tao-Tain-Do posture.

Ryan feinted with his right hand, seeing Michael react with lightning speed, already anticipating the blow from the left. The one-eyed man third-guessed him and followed through with the right, open-handed. The slap rang out, leaving the marks of the palm and fingers across the young man's smooth face.

Michael clenched his fists, ready to retaliate, but Ryan was already three steps away from him, near the sofa, hand hovering over the butt of his SIG-Sauer.

Doc threw down his knife and fork. "I'm not sure I care for your little lessons in power play, my dear Ryan. If the young man has erred, then it is only human. Surely it would be divine of you to simply forgive him?"

Ryan turned on the old man, the skin across his scarred cheek taut with anger. "Times you can say triple-stupe things and I let them pass, Doc. This isn't one of them."

"What did I do?" Michael sat again, picking up a slice of bread and smearing butter on it with fingers that trembled a little.

Ryan banged his fist on the table, making the mugs of coffee skitter sideways. "What did..." He spun on his heel and moved to the door, jerking it open and peering out into the deserted corridor. Their suite was in an angle of the building, with only one other room adjoining. He went to that door and yanked it open, finding the bedroom completely empty, without a stick of furniture. A large brown spider scuttled away, disturbed by his intrusion.

J.B. joined him in the passage, cradling his Uzi. "You thought..." he began.

"Wondered." He went back in and looked at Michael. "You knew there wasn't anybody listening at the door? Or in the room next door? Did you know that, boy? A nerve throbbed at Ryan's temple, just above his ruined eye. He kept opening and closing the fingers of his right hand, seething with tension and rage.

"No, I didn't. And I get what you mean, Ryan. You still didn't have to hit me."

"Wrong. Wrong in a mess of ways, Michael." With an enormous effort of will he succeeded in controlling himself.

It had been a long time since the crimson mist had flowed over his seeing and over his mind like that, and he realized, as he calmed a little, the strain that this expedition had put him under, leaving both his woman and his boy behind in the clutches of Baron Alferd Nelson.

At that moment Ryan decided that whatever happened in Yuma, he would probably chill the baron if they got safely back to Vista.

"You're nineteen, aren't you, Michael?"

"Yes, Ryan."

"You want to get to be twenty?"

"Sure."

"Then you have to think. Think all of the time. Not just when you're lying in a scrape in the dirt with fifty stickies charging at you. Any crazie can think at a time like that."

"I hear you, Ryan."

"No. That's what the slap was for. One of the best of Trader's sayings was that talk was cheap and that action costs. You might, *might,* remember next time, Michael. But Rosie Owen doesn't look to me like the sort of a lady you could trust further than you could throw a handful of dry vulture shit.''

"You suspect that our proprietor could have been eavesdropping, Ryan?" Doc said. "Upon my soul, I would not have suspected that."

Ryan smiled. "No, Doc, I guess you wouldn't. But I've lived a whole lot longer in Deathlands than you. One word to the baron here about our mission, and we'd all be dangling upside down over a slow fire, watching our own guts hissing and sizzling. So, we all keep quiet, all the time. Unless we're sure we can speak quietly without any risk."

"Someone's outside," Michael hissed.

Ryan nodded. "Capestrano and Ellie."

"How do you know?"

"Big man walking heavy and a woman in thin high heels."

There was a knock on the door.

"Come in."

Capestrano was a poem in pastels—a pale blue silk shirt, slashed to the navel, over lilac pants, tucked into soft cream boots. A large medallion had been slung around his neck, which Ryan decided was golden rather than gold. His hair was gelled with a scented pomade.

Ellie was with him, wearing a black shirt and midknee skirt. Her shoes were polished to a mirror finish, with three-inch heels.

"Good breakfast?" she inquired.

"Eaten worse," J.B. replied. "Only I can't recall when."

"We have been talking about what we should do for our performance here in Yuma." Capestrano glanced at Ryan.

"Tonight?"

"Ah, there is the rub. There lies in the heart and core of our dilemma. Ellie and I are as one in our feeling that it would be as well to seek a postponement until tomorrow."

Doc coughed. "I would personally hasten to second that suggestion."

"I'll third it," Michael said.

"It's just that we have suffered from a considerable depletion in our company," Ellie explained. "Diego and I have worked late last night and this morning on a reworking of one of our old favorites, so as to incorporate Doc and Michael to their best advantage."

"What is the name of this play, madam?" Doc asked, favoring the white-skinned woman with his most frightening smile, in which all of his huge and excellent teeth were well displayed.

Capestrano struck himself in the center of the chest, so hard that it made him cough. "We considered the finest examples of the dramaturge's art, throughout the ages."

Ellie continued. "We sadly rejected the Bard. Too many words."

Capestrano nodded again. "It was narrowed down to a choice between two smaller masterpieces."

"The first is *Both Handfuls*." Ellie smiled at Doc. "The tale of a dying gaudy whore who is saved by an older admirer who shoots her errant husband." She glanced at Capestrano. "And strangles her no-good son. You, Michael."

"Sounds okay to me," the teenager said.

"Older admirer?" Doc asked doubtfully. "What is the other choice?"

Capestrano turned on his megawatt beam. "A man of discernment, Doctor! I knew it. We have agreed on our other selection."

Ellie clapped her hands. "It involves some participation from the audience. Always popular. It is called *The Revenge*. A simple title. I will explain the plot as we go, but I am a maid left abandoned with a claim to the Matchless Mine. Diego is the villain who is attempting to steal both my virtue and my silver mine.''

"What part am I to play in this ingenious imbroglio, if I may be so bold as to ask?''

Ellie patted Doc on the arm. "My rescuer. And Michael is your oldest son. Knuckles is your younger son. A part that involves little speaking. And we capture all of Diego's cutthroats by a cunning subterfuge. It ends with Diego slain and me coupling with both of you at once.'' She looked around. "What do you all think?''

"The Revenge?" Ryan said. "Sounds a mighty good title for a play, Ellie. I have to go see the baron now, so I'll leave you to your practice.''

He closed the door on a strangely silent bedroom and stepped out into the cold, crisp Yuma morning.

Chapter Twenty-Five

As Ryan walked through the ville, he was conscious of a feeling that he'd had many times before. He always wondered what the place looked like before the nukes darkened the skies and thousands of millions died all across the globe.

He'd seen plenty of torn and bleached old magazines and broken books, as well as occasional scratched and jumpy vids, so he could formulate a sort of idea of Yuma, Colorado.

Tanned hunks of men in loose quilted parkas in vivid shades of purple and lime green would be escorting power-dressed blond women with perfectly cut manes and stiletto heels.

All of them would be locked into intricate games of buying and selling. People and things. And you hardly ever saw any of them within a half mile of the seductive slopes of fresh white snow.

Though you did see them in their wood-lined bedrooms laying out neat lines of fresh white powder on small silver mirrors.

There would be huge wags, dripping with

chrome and flake acrylic paint, rumbling along the sweeping curves of the interstates.

Now, Yuma didn't look much like that kind of rich-flavored ville.

Three-quarters of the original, prenuke buildings were gone, some folding up under seismic movements while many others had fallen victim to raging fires. Ryan looked around him as he walked, seeing that hardly any of the multistory accommodation blocks were still standing.

But many of the trendy boutiques that would once have formed part of a pedestrian mall were still there. Most of the windows were broken. Above the sagging or missing doors, Ryan could read the names, faded and almost obliterated by the weather, again, giving that odd, allusive flavor of the past: the Villa San Miguel, a Mexican restaurant, with two small green sombreros painted on either side of the window; Yuma Greenerie, the pictures showing an exotic flowering cactus, with a marijuana twining around it; Don Fernando's Casa de Yuma, with no clue to what that might have sold; Zapata the Jeweler; José's Veggie Eaterie.

The Arroyo Seco Bar and Gaudy. This was open and functioning, even that early in the morning. Ryan paused in the shadowy doorway, surrounded by the smell of last night's beer, cigarette smoke and vomit. A half-asleep girl at a round table caught his eye and beckoned to him.

"Want a breakfast quickie, mister?"

"No. Thanks, but no thanks. Too early in the day for me."

"Never too early for a good blowjob."

Ryan smiled. "Mebbe tomorrow."

"I'll be waiting." She kissed her ringed fingers and waved them to him.

"Hey."

"Yeah?"

"Going to report to the baron. Am I on the right road?"

"Sure. Past the corner of Daley and Manson. Can't miss it."

"Thanks."

She called after him as he walked on. "Hey there, One-Eye."

"What?"

"Make like you're walkin' on eggs when Sidler's in your face."

"Sure. Thanks."

THE YUMA Multiplex Cinema was easily identifiable. Partly because it was one of the biggest buildings left standing in the ville. Partly because there was a gang of ragged, slovenly sec men hanging around its front, like blowflies hovering over a haunch of rotting horse meat.

Ryan didn't recognize any of them from the previous day, though they were all obviously cast from the same unsavory mold.

All were male, mostly aged between twenty and forty, wearing a motley assortment of filthy and ragged clothes. All had the lightning flash in silver pinned to their jackets, and were mostly armed with automatic rifles, some with handblasters.

The old vid palace that squatted behind them was single storied, with a long frontage and a blank side wall of featureless gray concrete. A double door was open, showing only a cavernous blackness inside the building.

A tall man with a drooping mustache watched Ryan approaching and finally straightened up. "What do you want?"

"Outlander. New in the ville. Understand I have to see the baron."

"Right. Did the right thing. What's your name, mister?"

"Cawdor. I'm with the actors came in last night in the horse wag."

"You fucking the blond woman?" another of the sec guards asked.

"Not so's you notice it."

"The red-faced little prick doing her?"

"Wouldn't know. Haven't been riding with them that long."

"How about the kid with the big rad scar?"

"What about him?"

"He got a name?"

"Calls himself Knuckles."

There was a bellow of laughter from the group at that.

The man with the mustache appeared to be the leader, and he held up a hand to silence the noise. "Quieten it, brothers," he said. "Wizard doesn't like noise when he's viewing the vids."

"Means he *never* likes noise then," complained another guard.

"Can I go in?"

"How about leaving the blaster behind? Real pretty automatic that."

"I don't give up my blaster to anyone."

"Then you can't go in."

Ryan nodded. "Fine. Tell the baron I called but you wouldn't let me go see him."

An M-16 was jabbed hard into the small of his back. "Just give up that blaster, you fuckhead outlander!"

It was the one called Harve from the barrier on the highway, the same sec man that Ellie had succeeded in making look triple stupe in front of his companions.

"You going to pull the trigger, then do it, you mutie asshole! If you don't do it right now, then I'm going to take it away from you and ram it so far down your throat you'll be shitting full-metal jackets for a week."

Yet again, Ryan was aware of a blinding surge of anger. But the awareness did nothing to prevent it, and a small part of him found this a little worrying. But the larger part of him was relishing the confrontation and the risk, the feeling that he was actually doing something active, rather than just dancing to Baron Nelson's tune.

"Leave him be," said the guard with the long mustache.

Ryan turned and pushed the muzzle of the gun away from him, staring with bleak rage into the man's eyes.

"If you weren't going to meet Baron Sidler, I'd see to you," the sec man muttered.

"Be out soon enough, Harve. Then I'm still happy to talk to you some."

"Go on in. Before we have to clean some blood off the snow."

Ryan walked toward the doors, and it seemed as though he were instantly forgotten.

There were two braziers in the foyer of the old cinema, some of their smoke vanishing up into a pair of steel chimneys. But not all of it. A thick haze, piñon-scented, hung across the shadowy gloom.

Apart from a skinny black dog lying by the nearest fire, the large room was completely empty. As Ryan stepped slowly across the threadbare carpet, the animal stirred, whimpering. Its legs kicked for a moment as though it were dreaming of chasing rabbits in warmer days.

One wall was splintered, as though some sort of furniture had been ripped away from it, and a large patch of leprous damp fungus showed that the roof was giving up.

Several tunnels opened off the room. For some reason this kind of multiscreen movie house seemed to have survived in Deathlands better than buildings like schools or churches.

Ryan had seen several that had been almost perfectly preserved. The Russkies had used neutron missiles on the region, which slaughtered every living creature and left buildings unharmed.

So this cinema building didn't present any mystery to him.

He could hear sounds from one of the rooms, two along the branched passage, and flickering light seeped out from behind a set of heavy velvet draperies that partly closed off the entrance.

Ryan allowed his hand to drop to the butt of the SIG-Sauer, glancing behind him to make sure nobody was creeping up in the cold darkness to try to take him out.

The curtain smelled strongly of tobacco. It felt dry under his fingers, and he had the feeling that if he tugged at it, the material would open up like a banker's smile.

The voices grew louder, and he heard the noise of crackly and brassy music.

Ryan eased his way into what he recognized as the main auditorium of the cinema. There were rows of seats, some broken, some holding slumped figures. A swath of brightness sliced through, coming from a darkened box toward the back of the slope-floored room. At the front was a rectangular screen, carrying the pictures of the old vid.

It showed a strange glass-sided wag drawn by a couple of horses, moving up a steep hill, lined by frame houses. Two men rode the front of the rig, one in black. The other had a strange lopsided grin and was hefting a scattergun.

"Anyone want to bet some jack on them making it all the way to the graveyard and back again?" The voice was warm, cheerful and friendly, and sent a chill down Ryan's spine.

"You seen it a thousand times, Wizard," a voice from the far side of the theater complained.

"Sure I have. But I figure that some time it's

goin' to have a different ending. Know what I mean, Julio? Huh?''

Ryan paused, trying to accustom his eye to the gloom. Julio had been one of the names that Rick Coburn had mentioned back in Vista. One of the killers of the baron's son.

Something brushed against Ryan's leg, making him start. But it was only the mongrel, padding past him and heading toward the center of the front row.

The shotgun had boomed, blowing out a window on the side of the steep street. Ryan recognized the vid as being something that he knew was called a Western, though he'd never taken too much to the pleasure of watching moving films. Not that there were all that many left in Deathlands. Never mind the equipment to show them.

He leaned on the back partition and gazed at the scratched, jerky images. There was a standoff at the graveyard, then the rig came racing down the hill again, urged on by whoops from the dozen or so shadowy figures in the darkness of the auditorium.

The image suddenly vanished and the place went totally dark.

''I'll gut that fucking bastard!'' came the same warm and friendly voice. ''Letting it break. Put the lights on.'' The place was filled with a watery, yellowish glow from fittings around the walls. Heads turned immediately toward the stranger standing in the rear. "And just who the fuck are you, mister, coming in here to spoil our pleasure? Quick!"

"Name's Ryan Cawdor."

There was a very long silence.

Chapter Twenty-Six

The man in black was saying something about how only the farmers had been the winners. And that the gunmen had lost.

"We always lose."

Ryan glanced sideways.

Baron Wizard Sidler had whispered the dialogue of the whole vid, right the way through, laughing at every joke, weeping copiously when the tall skinny one with the knife got gunned down and when the half-breed with the slit eyes saved the lives of the little Mex boys and finished up getting himself chilled.

Now the memorable theme was pounding out and the cinema was filled with a general shuffling and moving about.

Ryan had been ordered to sit close to the baron, while one of his men struggled desperately to repair the antique machinery and get the film running again.

"You like vids, outlander?"

"Can't say that I've ever seen that many of them, Baron."

A man sat in the bucket seat next to Wizard Sidler, and Ryan's first impression was of the man's body odor. It wasn't the usual staleness of old sweat. It was a strange, brittle scent, like dry rotting wood.

The baron of Yuma was dressed like one of the characters in the vid that was showing. He'd even shaved his head to look like the one called Chris. The black shirt was too tight for him, and it barely stretched over his belly. Sidler had a pair of matched Navy Colts, worn in open holsters on each hip, tied low on the thigh. He looked to be about thirty years old.

Ryan had rarely met a baron in all of Deathlands who showed such friendliness and good nature. But he mistrusted Sidler. Not just because of what he knew about the man. Anyone who came on in such a warm and welcoming manner had to be a swift and evil bastard.

He already knew who Ryan was and all about the traveling theater company. He even offered them the cinema for their show.

"When will it be? Tonight?"

"Tomorrow, Baron."

"Ah, it will be interesting to see what a living vid is like."

There had been the shout of relief from behind them. "Ready to roll, Baron!"

"In a moment. Where did you come from, Cawdor? South?"

Ryan saw the danger. "More the east."

"You have not put your play on in the ville of Vista, have you?"

"No. Heard the name. Should we go there after we leave Yuma?"

Baron Wizard Sidler laughed and slapped Ryan on the thigh, his hand lingering there for a heartbeat longer than necessary.

"Vista is a place of poverty and cracked skin. Cold hearths and thin gruel. Stony bread and green bacon. Dry women and murderous men."

"And dead children, Wizard." The voice, strangely familiar, was from off to the left, where Ryan—his eye now adjusted to the gloom—had already spotted a group of five people sitting close together. It wasn't possible to be absolutely sure, but it looked to be four men and a single woman.

"Enough of that sort of talk, Jim." A colder note had entered the cheerful voice. "Zebe Nelson deserved his passing."

There was a long stillness in the dusty auditorium, eventually broken by the baron, his good humor restored, calling out for the vid to recommence.

AFTER IT WAS OVER, a slatternly woman with a hideous ulcer eroding one corner of her mouth brought in several tankards of good strong ale, offering them first to the baron, as was proper.

He took one, gesturing to Ryan to help himself, calling out to the others in the theater to come and refresh themselves.

"It's a long day's watching," he said.

Several of the people there were sec men, recognizable by the silver lightning flashes. But there were also the five that Ryan had noticed sitting in a tight group together.

The baron introduced them to Ryan as fellow outlanders.

"Passing on through, one day."

"One day," their leader echoed.

His name was Jim Jennison. Ryan figured him at around five-eight, lean and pale-faced. He squinted a little as though his sight were weak. All five wore better clothes than most of the inhabitants of Yuma ville. Much more like the way that Ryan and his group were dressed, including combat boots.

Jennison carried a double-action Heckler & Koch P-9S, nine round, 9 mm. Ryan noticed that the five had quality blasters, all of them in good condition. Again, a marked contrast to the filthy

guns that most of the baron's ragtag men trailed
around with them.

"Hi."

Ossie Grant was taller, with greased-back hair
and mismatched eyes, one blue and one a bright
emerald green. He had a bandolier with four throwing knives sheathed in it slung across his chest, and
a Model 58 Smith & Wesson Magnum on his right
hip. It had a blued finish and was in a decorative
border rig. He gave Ryan a disinterested smile.

"This is Julio. I don't know your other name,
Julio. Never did. What is it?"

"Just Julio does real fine, Baron," the teenager
replied.

With a name like that, Ryan would have expected him to show some signs of Mex ancestry,
but the boy was a well-built blonde with dazzling
blue eyes. He had on a flashy shirt in pale blue
silk, with dark blue piping around the throat. His
blaster was an unusual Texas Longhorn Border
Special, a single-action stubby little revolver that
held six rounds of what looked like center-fire .38s.
The boy also carried an unidentifiable sawed-down
scattergun, slung across his shoulders.

The fourth man had a mutie look to him. His
eyes were partly hidden behind a peculiar veil of
skin, like the wings of bees, and his long fingers
were webbed. As he grinned at Ryan he revealed

a triple row of needle teeth, with serrated edges to them. His hair was stringy, with no color to it. You couldn't say it was white or gray or brown.

Baron Wizard Sidler clapped the man on the shoulder. "This is Twenty Gooseneck. I can guess you're about to ask him how he came to have such an unusual name, weren't you, Ryan?"

"Yeah." He hadn't been.

"Well..." Sidler was unable to carry on. He was doubled over, his eyes popping with merriment, wheezing with gusts of laughter. "Truth is that the son of a bitch don't know!"

Gooseneck ignored the baron, simply moving a half step to one side, the hooded eyes watching Ryan with the unmistakable intensity of a serious traveling killer.

On his left hip was a Luna 300 target pistol, single-shot .22-caliber gun with an eleven-inch barrel and delicately adjustable sights. It was a specialist's weapon.

Balancing it on the right side was a powerful double-action Walther P-88 automatic, holding fifteen 9 mm rounds in the magazine. And, Ryan figured, a sixteenth round always slotted ready in the chamber.

Twenty Gooseneck was a very dangerous-looking individual.

"And this..." Sidler began, beckoning the woman.

But Jennison interrupted him. "Hold on a moment, Wizard."

Ryan noticed the total lack of respect in the way the pale man spoke to the ruler of Yuma ville, which was interesting.

"What, Jim?"

"We know this outlander's name. How about us hearing the names of all his party."

"They're just actors. I know who they are. Rest doesn't matter. You'll see them tomorrow night when they show us what they can do." He turned to Ryan. "They couldn't do a play of any of the great Randolph Scott vids, could they?"

Ryan didn't recall the name. "Don't know, Baron. I'll ask."

Jennison was still staring at Ryan. "I know you," he said quietly.

"Mebbe. Been around."

"One-eyed man. Carrying a good blaster with a look that shows he can use it. Has used it. Where've I seen you?"

Remembering a gesture from the vid they'd just watched, Ryan hitched a thumb to the north, then again to the south. And shrugged. "Anyplace, Jennison. Any place at all."

"You ever ride with the Trader?"

Ryan didn't hesitate for a second. "No. Heard of him. Had some war wags up in the Darks."

"And around."

"Rode with a Folsom."

"Yeah, Marsh Folsom."

"Didn't he get chilled by the Magus? The Warlock? Some name like that."

Jennison shook his head. "I heard he got chilled by Gert Wolfram, that blubbery freak-show guy, claimed he discovered stickies. But you never met this Trader, is that right?"

"Right."

"And you never met anyone called… Shit, no. Let it lie."

"Can I now meet you with the lady of the party, Ryan? Reena Miller."

There was a new note in Sidler's voice. It was the hot edge of lust, but there was also something that sounded like fear.

The woman spoke first. "You're asking yourself a question, Cawdor. All men do. Answer is always no. *Almost* always. Been watching you. Could be that the answer might, just might be Yes, if you want to ask it."

Reena Miller was something else. She was close to six feet with the blackest hair that Ryan had ever seen, a tumbling mane of silken midnight that fell almost to her waist, with a sheen that seemed to carry its own inner light.

Her eyes were close to gold, flecked with tiny motes of silver. She wore a black leather jacket over cream denim pants, tucked into black combat boots laced nearly to the knee.

Reena was wearing a nickel-finished Colt Cobra in a shoulder holster.

Ryan nodded to her, unable to think of anything to say. The cinema suddenly felt extremely cold, and he wanted to get back to the others.

He knew that he was in the presence of five seriously and competently evil bastards, and he'd realized how difficult his mission was going to be.

Chapter Twenty-Seven

The toy motorbike dated from well before the long winters. It bore a maker's name in Germany, and it was made from fragile tin.

Baron Alferd Nelson had wound it carefully with a flat key, turning a tiny knob between the handlebars to move a pointer on a dial, controlling what figures the blank-faced rider would execute.

"A double circle, Dean," he said, "like the number eight."

"I like the one when the two-wheel wag spins around and around."

They were kneeling together in a book-lined room close to the baron's own living quarters. The floor was rectangular blocks of polished sycamore, set in a diamond pattern. Nelson had laid his saber on a semicircular table beneath an oil painting of a tastefully ragged boy tending sheep by a gentle stream, where the yellow glow from the oil lamps was reflected off the hilt.

A gilt clock beneath a glass dome showed it was eight o'clock.

"We'll do that one next. Have to remove the back wheel for that, Dean."

"I know."

The clockwork mechanism whirred, and the toy whizzed around in its figure eight, the rider leaning over at a dangerously realistic angle.

Logs of sweet applewood crackled and spit in the hearth, behind the black mesh of the wrought-iron fireguard.

On a larger table there rested the remains of the meal that the giant and the child had eaten together an hour earlier.

Krysty's first reaction when Coburn brought the news that Baron Alferd Nelson desired to dine with Dean Cawdor was to refuse. But Mildred pointed out to her the danger of such a denial.

"He wants to whack us all, then he could've done it by now," she said.

The sec boss nodded his agreement. "It's true. Just that he misses his son, Zebe, more than you could imagine. Wants the lad's company." He turned to Dean. "The baron's got some real old, rare toys up there."

"Couldn't give a whistle up a pig's ass."

"Dean!" Krysty stabbed a finger at him angrily. "Rick Coburn's done nothing for you to be so rude."

"I don't mind."

Dean hunched his shoulders. "Sorry," he muttered. "But I don't like toys. Kiddie's shit."

"You might like these."

THE MEAL HAD BEGUN with a soup, rich and thick with great chunks of meat and vegetables. Some crusty bread went with it.

The baron had been very careful not to press the young boy with too much conversation too quickly.

There'd been some trout, boneless, in thin smoked strips for the second course, and then a game pie with creamed potatoes, carrots and mushrooms.

By then Dean had been eased into talking more, about himself, his mother, the way he'd been found by his father after the long empty years. But he was streetwise enough not to give away anything of any importance to his questioner.

The last course was delicious pieces of meringue, crispy and light, floating in a lake of rich golden custard.

"Sure you don't want some of this wine?"

"No, thanks."

"Good white zinfandel. Light and fresh."

"Happy with the milk, thanks."

Dean had drunk alcohol enough times in his eleven years to know that it was a potentially dangerous liquid. His mother, Sharona, had warned him to be careful not to allow a thief into his mouth that would try to rob him of his brains.

He'd always remembered that.

The boy had been nervous about the solitary evening with the towering man. The frail old lady that he knew was Nelson's mother had looked in on them around the middle of the meat pie. She'd sat in a deep brocaded armchair and said nothing, started crying silently and left as mysteriously as she'd come. Alferd Nelson had ignored her.

After the meal there had come the revelation of the toys.

Nelson had gone across to a huge cupboard that dominated one corner of the room. "This is where I kept everything for Zebe to play with."

There was an ancient padlock holding the closet shut. It had a faint green patina of age, and Nelson opened it with a key selected from a ring he wore at his waist.

Dean had gasped when he saw the treasure house revealed inside. His childhood had been notably low on toys and high on caution and death. But he was still boy enough to boggle at the cornucopia of wondrous goodies.

Everything was neatly stored and packaged.

Soldiers, made from wood and lead and plastic, wore uniforms from all ages and every country in the world. So it seemed to Dean as the baron ran a gigantic finger along the rows.

"Zouaves from far-off Dahomey and the French Foreign Legion. Grenadiers from Waterloo and the wily Pathan out of the Khyber Pass. Tennessee Volunteers and the Iron Brigade. Minutemen from Lexington and Rangers from Nam."

There was a wooden fortress that Nelson said doubled up for fighting against the cunning veiled Tuareg in the desert and against the Sioux in the Black Hills.

On higher shelves there were several sets of model trains and racing wags in bright colors. "Might get these out tomorrow, or the next day. Takes time to set the track and rails for them. Plenty of time. Your father's been gone three days. Still got seven more to go."

"That a war wag up there?" Dean pointed at a camouflaged armored vehicle with a long gun sticking from the turret.

"Main Battle Tank. The M-1 Abrams. One hundred and five millimeter cannon."

"Does it work?"

Nelson shook his head sadly, running his fingers through the expansive white beard. "No, afraid not, Dean. Used to be able to control it with some kind of wireless system. Never got it to work. Old skills they had before skydark."

He'd poured himself another large goblet of the pale pink wine, draining it almost without noticing it had gone.

That was when he'd produced the stunt motorcyclist from a torn box on the third shelf, handling it as though it were the Holy Grail.

Dean had loved it, entranced by the mechanical cunning of the old toy.

Finally the baron had stooped clumsily, swaying and nearly falling. He picked up the bike and replaced it in the closet, fumbling to snap the padlock shut.

"I'll do it," Dean offered.

"Think I'm drunk, do you, Zebe?"

"Not Zebe."

The deep-set eyes blinked owlishly at him from under the snowy lashes. "Not Zebe? Course not." The laugh was so forced it made the boy wince at the pain that lay behind it.

"Dean."

"I know."

"You sent my father off on a dangerous mission three days ago."

"I know that, too, boy."

Nelson sat heavily at the table, reaching out for the wine bottle and tipping it up, shaking it angrily when he discovered it was empty.

"Should I call for some more, Baron?"

"No. Had enough for tonight. Enough of you, Zebe. No!" The last word bellowed out like an angry lion.

"Want me to go?"

"Yeah. I want you to... No, I don't want you to go, boy. Don't want you to ever go. Want you to stay. Be my little boy. Be Zebe all over again for me."

"Can't be what I'm not." He remembered something that Krysty had said to Mildred a few hours earlier. "You can't raise the corn back up when it's in the barn, can you?"

The heavy head lifted toward him. "So wise, so young, Dean."

"Think I ought to go back to the others now. Thanks for the meal. It was good. And thanks as well for showing me the toys and stuff. It was real hotpipe, that two-wheeler."

"I mean no harm, boy. Not to you. To the two beautiful ladies who guard you. Not to your father and his friends."

"I know." The baron paused with his right hand on the ornately chased brass door handle.

The words came stumbling out, one at a time, with infinite spaces between them. "But, I tell you this, Dean. I...will...have...my...way!" The fists clenched, knuckles like carved bone. "By all the gods I will!"

Chapter Twenty-Eight

"Never give up the Matchless. My dear father's last words to me before he left for his final sad journey across the dark river. Never give up the Matchless, daughter." The words were followed by a heartrending sob.

"But you have no choice, my pretty maiden. No choice at all." Capestrano twirled an imaginary mustache as he sneered at her.

Ellie clapped a hand to her forehead. "There is always a— Oh, fuck it, Diego!"

"Want a prompt?"

"Want something to get rid of this buggering headache."

"Perhaps the stuffiness of this room?" Doc suggested.

"No. Get them a lot. Like someone's got their thumb stuck behind each eye, trying to push them out of their sockets."

Ryan lay on the bed, watching the rehearsal, with J.B. perched on the sofa on the other side of the bedroom.

The Revenge didn't seem to have very much shape to it. So far it was Ellie and Diego, strutting and declaiming, while Doc and Michael shared a crumpled and much rewritten script. Knuckles was content to squat quietly in the corner, occasionally allowing the tip of his forefinger to caress the livid rad scar on his left cheek.

Ryan had reported back to the others after his morning's viewing of the old vid and his meeting with the baron. J.B. had been very interested in the description of the four men and a woman who were their targets.

"You heard of any of them?"

The Armorer slowly shook his head. "Still not sure. I'd mebbe need to see them, Ryan. But if I'm right, then seeing them could be the worst thing. Finish us all off."

Diego Capestrano turned toward them. "Could you possibly keep the noise down? You're preventing the artistes from readying a brilliant and memorable performance for tomorrow night."

"Not tonight?"

"Tomorrow. Then it will be wonderful." He threw his arms around Doc and Michael. "We will *all* be wonderful."

THEY BROKE FOR LUNCH, served in the big room by Rosie Owen. Her puffy face, heavily made up, was a mask of curiosity.

"You outlanders going to put on this vid in the baron's place?"

"On the morrow," Capestrano replied.

"Lots of folks real interested," she said, pausing in the doorway, one hand reaching inside her blouse to scratch at herself.

J.B. stood from the chair by the window. "Who?"

"Sidler's five killers. Couple of them been around this morning."

Ryan looked across at his old friend, then back to the landlady. "What did you tell them?"

She smiled, showing what looked like a chunk of cabbage leaf stuck between her uneven front teeth. "Said your business was your business. Did I do right, mister?"

Ryan nodded. "Yeah," he said. The door closed. "Bitch'd sell out her baby daughter if the price was right," he said quietly.

To his amazement, by the time the sun was setting over the gray expanse of snow-wiped mountains all around Yuma, *The Revenge* was beginning to take a real sort of shape.

Capestrano was skilled enough to know that amateurs like Doc and Michael couldn't possibly cope with long speeches. So he and Ellie took the burden of the business.

"So you think that I should stand up to the evil devil that seeks to steal my inheritance? And you and your two sons will help me with a plan to defeat him and his gang?"

That was Ellie.

"Yes."

That was Doc.

The old man shook his head in admiration. "This is putting words in someone else's mouth with a real vengeance, my dear Ellie. I believe that the entire sixty minutes of drama involves me in little more than a dozen brief utterances."

"Never mind, Doc," she said, touching him lightly on the arm with a fan made from tattered osprey feathers. "Maybe I can make it up to you."

"Oh, I'm not complaining, dearest lady. The less this poor befuddled old pate has to hold, the better for all of us."

THE TRADER USED TO HAVE a number of rules, though none of them were carved in marble. In fact none of them were written down at all. But most of the crews of the war wags knew them.

One related to frontier pestholes like Yuma.

"Get in slow and careful. Get out quick and

careful. While you're there, keep quiet and careful."

It was claustrophobic all being together in the boarding house. The sky had cleared in the afternoon, and the ville looked almost tempting. Capestrano was keen that the rehearsals should carry on through, and Ryan was content that none of them should leave the place.

In the evening, it began to snow again, dusting the streets and roofs.

Everyone took a break while supper of mutton stew was served. Afterward Ryan decided to risk a walk around the ville.

"Coming, J.B.?"

"No."

"Anyone else?"

"Me?" Knuckles turned quickly to Capestrano, seeking approval.

"Why not? You've done well this afternoon and you know the play. Yeah, go and have a breath or two of what passes for fresh air in this stinking burg. Be back in an hour. I want to work before we all retire to our beds on the scene where the wretched villains are lured into the trap."

"How's that done with just the five of us?" Michael asked.

"Audience participation is the name we professionals use." Ellie flounced to the sofa where Doc was sitting and leaned forward with a coquettish wink and a toss of her hips. "How about you, my dearie?"

"I beg your pardon?"

"That's what I say to the seaters. What we call the audience. I tempt them up onstage. Just five or six, to play the villain's men. All they have to do is stand around and look mean, magnificent and very moody."

"Then?" Ryan asked.

"Out the back door where the plot says they get taken prisoner. They really go around the front and into the theater in plenty of time for the rude ending with me, Doc and Mickey here."

"There is a rear exit to the Multiplex, is there, Ryan?" Capestrano asked. There was no answer. The one-eyed man was staring across the bedroom, a preoccupied expression on his face. "Ryan?"

"Sorry, Diego?"

"A rear exit?"

"How's that?"

Ellie tweaked Ryan's unshaved cheek. "Wake up in there. Anyone home?"

"I was miles away."

"Thinking about Krysty, Dean and Mildred?" Michael asked.

"No. A rear exit from the vid house? That what you asked me?"

"Indeed."

"Think so. There looked like ways off the stage on both sides. Figures there must be a way out the back of the building. I'll check it out."

But he was still not entirely with them. The melodramatic climax to the play had given Ryan the germ of a plan for capturing the killers without there being too much risk of a direct confrontation with Sidler's sec men.

KNUCKLES WAS HUDDLED inside a thick blue-and-green plaid trench coat, which concealed the tilted hump of his shoulder. He seemed delighted to be out with Ryan, scuttling along at his side, a short-hafted tomahawk tucked into a sheath on his left hip.

"Real cold snow," he said.

"Yeah. Going to get a lot colder as winter closes in."

"Why you're not in the play? You and Mr. Dix? Good feeling, the play."

"You been with Capestrano and Ellie for very long, Knuckles?"

"Sure. Since I was little. Man in Darks had me. Wanted to cut me and change my face for a freakery. Capestrano won me off him at five-card draw. Aces and eights."

The gaudies were busy, with the noise of music

and tuneless singing, an occasional scream and, once, the sound of breaking glass. There was a wicked wind slicing through the pass to the north of Yuma, carrying shards of ice in its teeth, more than enough to sweep the alleys and streets of the ville bare of life. There wasn't even a dog to be seen.

"Going look around back the place? See there's way out for end of the play?"

"Sure. This way. Corner of Manson and Daley. Not far."

Ryan lifted his hands and blew into them, feeling the cold seeping into his joints, wondering for a moment how things were back in Vista. This was the night of the third day. The first performance was the night of the fourth day. Allow two days to get back again. Only left them...

"Four days," he said, not even aware he'd spoken out loud.

"What is, Ryan?"

"Nothing, Knuckles." He rubbed his good eye, watering in the norther. "There's the place where Wizard Sidler hangs out."

The young man drew back into the shadows, peering at the Multiplex. The rad scar that distorted his left eye was illuminated by a red lamp fixed to the wall just above his head.

"Don't like look that place, Ryan," he muttered. "Could be I'll go back to rehearse."

"What's wrong, Knuckles?"

"I be seeing darkness, Ryan."

"You a doomie?"

"No. Just sort of feel place is bad."

"You'd help me if you came along. Watch my back in case some bastards try and coldcock me in the alley there."

Knuckles shook his head slow. "I be waiting here for you."

"Sure." There was no point in trying to force Knuckles to accompany him around the rear of the building. Be much worse than doing it alone. "Just wait here. Or would you rather go on back to the others? I don't mind."

"Stay here, Ryan."

"Good."

The usual gang of sec men were gathered around the front of the multiscreen cinema, but they were far too busy watching a fight between two drunken gaudy sluts on the far side of the street, in front of a bar called the Black Raven.

Nobody took any notice of the well-built man with the single chillingly pale blue eye as he picked his way over a pile of broken bottles into the short, shadowed passage that ran along the back of the Multiplex.

Ryan saw a single small window on the second story, its glass shattered and repaired with a piece of water-stained veneer. It was far too high to reach and would only offer entry to someone as slim and agile as Dean.

He set that thought aside and walked farther into the pitch darkness. His feet slipped on what might have been mud or shit or slush, and he nearly stumbled, steadying himself with a hand against the concrete wall of Sidler's HQ.

There was something protruding from the ice-slick stone, a little above head height. A broken sign. There was a momentary rift in the oppressive layer of leaden cloud, giving just enough light for him to read the lettering.

What remained of it—''gency,'' and below the single word ''it.''

''Emergency exit,'' Ryan whispered, feeling a faint glow of pleasure that he'd identified it.

It was a double door, held closed by a rusting chain and a battered padlock. Ryan guessed that nobody in Yuma was going to be triple-stupe enough to try to break into the back entrance of the baron's own personal fortress.

From what Diego Capestrano had said, this could be fine for the climax of their play. There had to be a way off the stage into this alley. If it was tidied up a little, there would be room to drive a horse wag along it.

"Yeah…" Ryan breathed, his narrow lips peeling back in the beginnings of a vulpine smile.

His acute hearing was numbed by the cold and the whispering of the blue norther. The first warning he had of the attack was when something drove into him brutally hard, just above the kidneys, knocking him gasping to his knees.

Chapter Twenty-Nine

Even before he hit the dirt, Ryan's combat reflexes were taking over, going into an automatic response, diving forward and rolling on his right shoulder, his mind riding over the savage pain in his lower back.

In the second or so it took him to come up into a fighting crouch, Ryan had figured out that there were two attackers, one who'd hit him with what looked in the darkness like a baseball bat, the other holding a steel blade that glinted in the reflected splinters of moonlight.

It was impossible to make out any details, except that they were good. They'd come up quietly enough to take Ryan completely by surprise, and that meant real good.

They were also fast enough to follow up on him, giving him no chance to draw the SIG-Sauer from its holster.

The bat hissed through the air, and he managed to roll away, his feet slipping on a mixture of ice and broken bottles.

"Bastard!" the attacker hissed, his breath feathering white around his face.

Ryan fumbled for the panga on his hip, but again he had to throw himself away from the pounding length of wood.

"Let me blast him."

"Jennison said no noise, you shithead stupe!"

Ryan filed away the fact that one of the five had sent assassins after him, wondering if he'd live to make use of the information.

To buy himself a moment Ryan scooped up a handful of the frozen mud and glass and hurled it into the face of the nearer of the attackers, hearing the man cry out in shock and take a panicky, involuntary step backward.

If Jennison, the pale, squinting leader of the gang of killers, had set him up, then the sound of a shot might attract him to the alley.

Ryan went for the eighteen-inch steel blade of the machete instead. He gripped the hilt and powered himself up off the floor of the back alleyway, watching for the swing of the baseball bat again, ready to try to jink to the side.

But the man was off balance, not expecting to find his scrambling victim coming at him with an enormous knife gleaming in his fist.

Ryan jabbed at the assassin's throat with the

point, feeling it penetrate flesh, bringing a yelp of pain. But it wasn't a fatal wound.

Wasn't intended to be.

Ryan knew that the man's instinctive reaction would be to snatch at the gash in his neck, feeling to see how badly he was hurt. There would be the warm wetness of blood on his fingers, a mixture of horror and shock clouding his mind.

The panga swung across Ryan's body and he tensed himself, ready to put all of his strength into the backhanded blow, aimed at his attacker's lower stomach and groin.

It worked perfectly.

The honed edge slashed through the thermal jacket, through the shirt and through the double-layered winter vest beneath. Through skin, flesh and muscle.

The man gave a strangled, inarticulate gasp of terror and pain. Blood flooded out from the gaping wound, hot across Ryan's hand, dappling the blade of the panga and pattering noisily into the icy slush around their feet.

"Oh, fuck. He's done me..." The cry was high and thin, like that of a smacked child.

Ryan didn't hesitate.

In front of him he could see that the would-be murderer was on his knees, arms wrapped around the leaking wound in his belly, clutching himself

as though he could prevent his life from soaking
away into the dirt.

"Do him...." Venom overlaid the pain in the
voice.

Ryan heard the sound of steel on stone as the
second of the attackers dropped his knife. But the
one-eyed man was concerned only with finishing
the man who knelt, helpless in front of him.

The panga swept up and back, shoulder-high,
coming around in a lethal arc of pure power, all of
Ryan's strength going into it.

Ryan felt a slight jar, then a harsher, grinding
jolt that ran clear up his right arm. The blade hesitated, held for a moment, then it was through the
bony obstruction. On and out, clear through the
other side of the man's muscular neck.

Ryan stepped back, shielding himself from the
fountain of arterial blood that jetted eight or ten
feet high into the blackness. He heard the solid
clunk as the severed head rolled against the back
wall of the cinema.

"What the fuck... Oh, blessed saints!"

Despite his appalled horror, the second attacker
managed to keep his nerve. There was the distinc-
tive click of a blaster's hammer being thumbed
back.

Ryan was aware that what little light illuminated
the alley was behind him, turning him into a prime,

silhouetted target for the murderer. And he was a good seven or eight paces away from the barrel of the gun, too far to try anything and too close for the man to miss him.

"Jim Jennison didn't pay you to let everyone in Yuma know I've been chilled," he said.

There was nothing. No bullet. No response. Just nothing.

"Walk away and it won't happen," he tried. "Just do it."

"Fuck you." The voice was calm and controlled. "You cut off my brother's fucking head and tell me to walk away. Nobody orders me to walk away. Nobody."

"Tell me something."

"What?"

"Why did Jennison pay you and your brother to have me put away?"

"Fuck you."

But the man still didn't fire.

"Got to be a reason. Cost your brother his life already."

"Just fuck you, outlander. You're the one-eyed man, aren't you?"

"Yeah. Why?"

"Wasn't supposed to be you. Not so much jack for you."

Ryan inched a half step forward. He thought

he'd seen a hint of movement behind the dark shape of the man with the gun. His immediate guess was that it was Jennison, coming to check up on how his jack had been spent.

"What do you mean? Listen, this doesn't have to be, man."

There was a tremble in the voice that came out of the velvet shadows. "Has to be now. If you hadn't done that..."

"Who did Jennison say he really wanted nined by you?"

"Don't fucking matter now."

"Still interested."

"Jennison paid us to chill any of you. But most of—"

There was a wet thud. Ryan's immediate thought was that it sounded like a sharp ax slicing into a rotting mangrove tree.

Which was about half right.

A second sound followed on the heels of the first, which seemed like a sigh, as if someone had just slid into a warm bath after a heavy day.

Which wasn't anywhere near right.

A gun clattered on the ice-slick stones of the alley, and then the heavy noise of a dead man slumping to the earth.

"Knuckles?"

"Came after you. Nearly too late. Sorry, Ryan. Got him with my tomahawk."

"That's good. If you'd been with me, they might have taken us both at once. You did right." He paused. "Just a shame you didn't let him go on living a few seconds longer. He was about to tell me something interesting. Never mind."

"Sorry about that, Ryan." Knuckles sniffed. "Just saw danger. Me was real scared."

Ryan grinned. He stooped and wiped the blade of the panga on the jacket of the nearer corpse, then resheathed it.

"Well, we found the back door of Sidler's fortress, all right."

Knuckles shuffled in. "Could me have the blaster, Ryan?"

"Sure. But keep it out of sight, or we're in deep shit. Someone sees you with it and recognizes it, Knuckles..." Ryan allowed the warning sentence to trail off into the cold evening.

"We go back now?"

"To the warm splendor of the Snow Palace? Sure. Let's go."

"We just leave dead men?"

"They won't mind, Knuckles. They're past minding anything."

The hunchback laughed. "That's real good joke, Ryan. Me sure like that."

He was still laughing when they got safely back
to their rooms.

RYAN WASN'T at all surprised that the killing of
the two men in the alley produced no sort of come-
back. There was no visit from sec men. When Rosie came up in the morning with the maid carrying
their loaded breakfast trays, she never even mentioned the deaths.

Frontier pestholes like Yuma were places where
life was cheap and the dying was all too easy.

Chapter Thirty

The fourth day out of their allotted ten was also spent on intensive rehearsals.

Ryan had finally decided to mention to J.B. that one of the putative assassins had said that Jim Jennison had paid them to take out any of the outlanders, but that their prime target hadn't actually been Ryan himself.

"They say who he wanted to hit?"

"No."

"Me?"

Ryan was sitting by the window, speaking quietly, while behind them Ellie was enthusiastically readying herself for the climactic scene in which she enjoys sexual relations with both Doc and Michael. The teenager was proving shy and stubborn, but Doc was flinging himself into the part with great abandon.

"Didn't say. But from the way you been acting, J.B., I'd have thought it was likely."

The Armorer tugged back the corner of the faded plastic-lace curtains, glancing out into the morning's dull light. The wind had risen to near gale force, carrying hail and sleet with it, the pellets of ice pattering against the glass.

"Could be," he agreed finally.

"You know this Jennison? Or someone else in the gang?"

J.B. turned back, removing his glasses and wiping them. "Seems more likely. Trouble, there's only one way I can be certain. That's by going out there. And if I'm right, then it could be time for us to hit the graveyard shift."

And that was all he'd say.

AFTER THE NOON MEAL of bread and cheese, with slightly rancid butter, Monsignor Diego Capestrano was readying his augmented company for their first performance of *The Revenge*.

"Perhaps you and J.B. could be our audience," he suggested.

"I've got to go see the baron again," Ryan said. "Fix up the stage and make sure that rear door's cleared for use."

Ellie pouted at him. "Then you won't see me in all my pomp, Ryan." She closed her eyes and shook her head, sucking in a breath.

"What's wrong?"

"Nothing, dear heart. Just a spasm of pain behind the eyes. I get it sometimes. First-night nerves they used to call it in the olden days. The greatest stars in the Hollywood and Broadway firmaments used to suffer from it. So they say. It'll go. Always goes.'' And she smiled.

But Ryan had seen the reality of the hurt, and he wondered again about Knuckles's rad scar. Deathlands was still a patchwork of dangers. Hot spots scattered around from the long-life nukes still had an ability to deal out rad cancers.

As he left, they were still playing the opening scene, where Ellie, newly an orphan, was leaning her head on a table, bemoaning her poverty and explaining to the audience all the prequel plot about being left the Matchless Mine.

Diego was waiting to enter and offer her salvation from her mortgage and her worries. But only at a dual price—her honor and her gold mine.

Or was it a silver mine? Ryan couldn't quite remember which.

As he clattered down the main staircase of the Snow Palace he wondered again about Jim Jennison and the link with John Barrymore Dix.

He made his way outside to check the livery stables, filling his lungs with the sweet scent of summer hay bursting from the loft.

Capestrano's wag was safe, with their horse comfortably quartered in one of the row of twenty or so stalls. Ryan wanted to make certain that the rebuilt Conestoga rig could, if necessary, be pulled by a pair of horses. And that there were other draft animals there.

Their own mounts were also in the stable, the burro baring its tombstone teeth at him as he leaned over the partition.

"BARON'S ILL."

"What's that?"

"Ill. You fucking deaf, are you, outlander? He's ill."

"What with?"

"Go ask him yourself. How should I know? Ill. What's that mean, anyway?"

"Bad?"

The sec man shook his head so hard it dislodged the silver lightning flash from his jacket and he had to bend to pick it up.

"Wizard Sidler doesn't come around and whisper in my fucking ear when he gets a dose or a cough or a boil on his ass!"

Ryan kept his patience. "I just want to know when he'll be okay enough for me to see him. We need his say-so on the play tonight inside there."

The sec man laughed contemptuously, but Ryan hung on to his self-control and resisted the temptation to ram the SIG-Sauer into the man's mouth and break off a few teeth.

"Won't be no fucking play tonight. Tell you that right now. So you can fuck off and not keep us all here in the fucking cold."

"Baron said it was his decision. Said to make sure I spoke to the hunter and not one of his bastard snapping mongrels."

The man looked at him. There were half a dozen of the guards standing around the entrance to the lobby of the Multiplex. Ryan noticed at that moment that the tall Ossie Grant was at the rear of the group, making himself inconspicuous. The narrowed eyes, one blue and one green, were fixed on his face. In the shadows Ryan spotted the man's right hand was resting casually near the butt of his Smith & Wesson revolver.

"Outlander, you just finally—" The sec man stopped as Grant interrupted him.

"Not a good idea."

"You hear what he called..."

"Get on with it."

"Why don't you speak direct to me, instead of acting like a bastard ventriloquist, Grant? Seems there's an awful lot of pigs dipping their snouts into the baron's trough."

The killer ran his fingers through his greasy hair. "Some right in what you say, Cawdor. But you better watch your mouth in Yuma. Not always the baron calls the tune here."

Ryan eyed the man. "I hear you, Grant. But it's simple. Sidler agreed we'd show him the play. Here, tonight. If he's ill, we can do it tomorrow. Not a problem."

"Or the day after."

"Sure."

"He's got a bad cough and throat. Gone to his chest this morning."

Ryan was aware of movement deeper inside the building, and he thought he could make out the cream jeans of Reena Miller, wondering if someone there had a bead drawn on him.

The first of the sec men laughed at Grant. "Hurt his throat whooping and hollering when big John and ugly Lee start slugging it out."

Ryan turned away, then remembered. "Don't forget. The back door. Have it cleared away and opened. And have the alley tidied up. Need it for the play. All right?"

"Who the fuck—" Ossie Grant laid a hand on the sec man's shoulder, the fingers tightening. "Don't do... That fucking hurts me, man."

"Do like the outlander says. His lips move, but it's Wizard's voice you hear." Grant smiled thinly at Ryan. "That door was found to be blocked only this morning, Cawdor."

"Yeah?"

"Yeah." The smile broadened. "Now, I'm interested that you aren't interested."

"I couldn't give a flying buffalo fart for what you're interested in, Grant."

The figure in the gloom had moved to one side, vanishing.

"You want to know what blocked off that door in the alley, Cawdor?"

"No." He took a half step toward the man, nodding to himself as Grant backed off. "But I know you're going to tell me."

"Sure am. It was a couple of stiffs. And after a night in the open I surely mean that they were real stiff!"

"So? You saying that I came out here in the snow and murdered two men? Why would I do that, Grant? Unless some jack had changed hands?"

"How do you figure that?" But the charge had gone home. He was blinking, turning to look behind him as though he were expecting some sort of signal from the darkness.

Ryan shook his head. "I'm not going to play your triple-stupe games. Make sure that place is ready for when the baron gets well again." He pointed a finger between Grant's eyes. "And tell him I hope that's real soon. Don't forget. Your responsibility. Yours. Not mine."

He walked away, raising his hand to brush away a salt tear that had leaked from behind his eye patch, the raw socket irritated by the chilly wind. Ryan didn't look back.

THE NEWS of the postponement was greeted with mixed reactions. Diego Capestrano seemed pleased, clapping his chubby hands. "Extra time to hone and polish our performances! Excellent."

Ellie had mixed feelings. "I think we'd have been ready to go tonight, Diego," she said. "But I guess a little more time won't hurt. Long as we don't get too polished and jaded."

Doc laughed. "I think that is an unlikely scenario, my dear lady. Something as old and rough as myself can scarcely suffer from being too smoothly polished, I think."

She reached up on tiptoe and kissed him on the cheek. "You always put yourself down, you old bear. There's many a fine tune comes from an old piano. Isn't there, Doc?"

Ryan was amused to see a slight blush suffuse Doc's grizzled face. "I suppose there is some evidence to support that hypothesis, my dear. The finest wines are the oldest."

"Until they turn sour, Doc." Michael grinned.

J.B. was the least happy. "Puts us into the fifth

day, Ryan," he said, as the two of them stood by the window.

"Can't be helped. Just have to hope that Baron Sidler gets himself better quickly. We got a safety margin. But we have to be away by the evening of the eighth day. Or it's all up for Krysty, Mildred and Dean."

Chapter Thirty-One

Rosie Owen brought in their breakfast the next morning on a battered wooden cart.

"Here's some lovely leftover pork chops I got cheap from me sister who does cooking down at the Buck'n Doe gaudy on Lector Avenue. Fried them up with some turnip greens and okra. Did some eggs over-easy on the top, but I don't think they was kind of...well, as fresh as I thought they was. Still, it's all food, isn't it? Goes in one end and before you know it there's just a splattered mess down the shitter."

She smiled at the assembled company and went back into the hallway.

J.B. was first to look at what she'd brought in.

"A splattered mess down the shitter," he repeated quietly, shaking his head. "But it looks like that already."

A large green-and-white platter stood in the center of the cart, and it looked like seven chunks of greasy and charred meat rested on the plate. A small mound of melted, soggy greens glowered in one corner, with what had to be the over-easy eggs heaped on top. The yolks resembled dulled, golden bullets while the whites were semiliquid, dappled with burned grease and speckled with fragments of broken shell.

A crock of butter and half a loaf jostled each other in one corner, while a large blue enamel pot of coffee stood steaming gently in the opposite corner.

"Coffee smells good," Knuckles said.

"And half a loaf is better than none," Doc added.

Despite its disgusting appearance, the food didn't actually taste that bad. The scorched fat succeeded in overwhelming even the sour taint of the past-their-best eggs.

"Had worse," J.B. pronounced, wiping the last smears of sticky grease from his plate with a hunk of dry bread, washing it all down with a gulp of sweet black coffee.

Ryan nodded his agreement. "Remember that crazy old bastard in…what was it called? By that broken-down dam? Sunbake! That was it."

"Sure. Used to boast that he had one ear, one tooth, one hand, one leg and the biggest cock west of the Pecos." J.B. grinned. "And he'd lay it on the table to show you if you didn't believe what he said."

Ellie gasped. "That's awful." She paused. "And was it?"

The Armorer nodded. "Have to say that it was."

Ryan carried on the tale. "Went all the way mad. Served Trader a meal once that had everything kind of backward. Would've made Rosie here seem the finest cook in the damned world." He shook his head. "Poured away the coffee and served cups of hot grounds. Fried up the rinds of the bacon and the shells of the eggs. Peel of oranges rammed in the glasses, instead of the juice."

"Threw out the contents and put empty cans on the table." J.B. whistled. "Yeah. Have to say that was about the worst."

"What did the Trader do?" Michael asked. "Bet he got mad."

"No." Ryan shook his head reminiscently. "Trader never got mad. He just got even."

"So, what did he do? Probably blew the guy apart with his blaster."

J.B. leaned back in his chair. "No. Just made him eat it all himself. Everything except the cans."

The teenager laughed. "Taught him a real lesson, I bet."

Doc had heard the story before. "It all depends on what you mean by learning a lesson, young man. Later that day I believe that the poor wretch went to his barn and climbed into a bath of gasoline, then opened the veins in his wrist. Couldn't even get the details right of taking his own life. Was that the lesson you had in mind?''

Michael didn't answer him.

At that moment the door suddenly snapped open again, making everyone jump.

Rosie stuck her head around it. ''Y'all finished with the food?'' There was a muttered chorus of reluctant agreement. ''That's good. I'll clear it all up and let you get on with practicing your play. Just don't make no mess nor dirt in my good rooms.''

With a clattering of crockery she was gone, the sound of the squeaking cart diminishing down the corridor.

Ellie ran a finger along the sill of the window, holding it out, black with sticky dust. ''Just don't make no mess nor dirt in my good rooms,'' she mimicked.

Less than five minutes later the landlady was back.

''Thought you'd like to know.''

''What is it? You must not burst in on us like this, without even the minimal courtesy of knocking and waiting.''

''Oh, sorry I'm even fucking living!''

Capestrano tutted impatiently. ''Well, you're here now. What is it?''

"Thought you'd like to know."

"You already said that. Please tell us what it is that you think we'd like to know. Then we can decide whether we'd like to hear it. Or not. As the case may be."

Now the woman looked confused. She stuck her finger in her ear and wobbled it vigorously. "Ah, that's better. Now, do you want me to tell you this, or not?"

"Yes. For pity's sake tell us this news, sweet madam. Or should I prostrate myself and press my lips to the toe of your shoe?"

"If you want to, mister. I had a customer once wanted me to drink half a gallon of beer and then, when I was bursting, sit on—"

Ryan drew the SIG-Sauer and cocked it. "Ten seconds to tell us, then get out."

"Sec man said that Baron Sidler's still real sick. Coughing blood." The words tumbled over one another in her haste to spit them out.

"Fine." Ryan holstered the blaster. "Good you told us. Now you can go."

Her face had lost its color when he pointed the automatic at her. Now she swallowed hard. "Right. I'll do that."

"Close the door quietly."

"Yeah, yeah."

They waited until they heard her down-at-heel men's boots clumping toward the stairs.

J.B. spoke first. "Puts us through to the sixth day, Ryan."

Capestrano clapped his hands. "I think that it's well past time that you told us a little of this strange mission you four have here in Yuma, and why the passing of the days is so significant." He seated himself on one of the beds. "I'm waiting."

You stay alive in Deathlands by not trusting anyone at all. But there were times that you had to take others into your confidence, times you needed someone to watch your back, times you actually needed help.

Times that you could no longer stand alone.

Ryan trusted Krysty and J.B., and Doc when his mind wasn't off wandering down Victorian byways. He'd come to trust Mildred, and his young son.

Michael Brother was still very much on probation, but he was getting there.

Now there was the question of whether to tell the truth to Capestrano, Ellie and Knuckles.

Ryan came at it from another direction.

Could they afford not to tell them?

AFTER HE'D FINISHED talking there was a long stillness in the stuffy bedroom. Ellie looked across at

Capestrano, but neither of them spoke.

Knuckles coughed to attract attention. "All right me say something?"

"Sure," Ryan said. "Go ahead. We're all in this together. What happens to one of us'll happen to all of us."

"These killers. You sure they done what you say they done?"

Ryan nodded. "Far as I know. There's no such thing as truth, Knuckles. We all see things in a different way. See different truths. But I think they did. Yeah, I believe it."

"You do this if you didn't believe it?"

It was a surprisingly shrewd question. Ryan hesitated for several heartbeats. Would he be responsible for the deaths of others to try to save the lives of those he loved?

"Yeah. But I'd feel bad about it, Knuckles. That's an honest answer."

Ellie stood and walked to the door, opening it an inch and peering into the corridor. "Nobody there," she said, smiling weakly. "Getting suss about things now you've told us this."

"Is it vital that we are involved in your kidnapping?" Capestrano asked.

J.B. answered him. "No."

"Then why—"

"Haven't finished."

"I beg your pardon."

"No, you don't have to be involved. But if we get away from here with Sidler, or the others, then you either come with us or you stay here and you get burned. Just because of knowing us. Sorry, but that's the way it is."

The rosy-cheeked man nodded, solemn. "I see that. I see you could have done what you had to, and then fled and left us to face the displeasure and wrath of the audience. Yes, we will do what we can. And afterward, we shall make our excuses and depart with you."

BARON WIZARD SIDLER was no better the next day, still suffering from a racking cough and a raging fever, unable to eat or drink.

Time was moving faster and faster.

Chapter Thirty-Two

Dr. Theophilus Tanner was exhausted. He had a sick headache, and the constant supply of grossly appalling food from Rosie Owen's kitchen meant he was suffering a permanent burning feeling of nauseous indigestion.

The original idea of appearing in a theatrical entertainment had seemed whimsical and droll.

Now it simply terrified him.

He'd had a vivid dream the night before that still gave him a cold chill at his nape.

It had been prompted, Doc imagined, by the rehearsals they'd had during the sixth day away from Vista ville. Despite his illness, Baron Sidler had granted them permission to work out their moves on the actual stage where they'd do the show. And, to Ryan's relief, had arranged for the rear exit and the alley out back to be cleared away.

To Capestrano's relief, the baron had also agreed to pay a portion of their fee in advance.

But performing on the stage had enveloped Doc in a rash of pure terror.

And the dream focused that fear.

He'd been waiting in the wings, ready to appear in his first-ever play, which had been nothing like *The Revenge*. It was a Restoration comedy, brimming with elegant gallants and mannered fops. Doc knew that he had only a single line to say, but it was vital to the plot. Wearing a tall wig and frocked coat, he had to stride into the middle of some sort of party and declare "But, my lord, that syphilitic son of a sea cook was actually the Bishop of Bath and Bunnham."

His moment was coming closer. Around the fringed dusty curtain he could glimpse the rows of pale, eager faces in the audience.

His cue was one of the court ladies striking a lace-festooned macaroni on the wrist, saying, "La, my Lord Wackham, but this wogue sounds a wather wicked wascal."

Here it came.

In his dream-turned-nightmare, Doc took a shallow breath and walked onto the raked boards, blinded for a moment by the bright floods.

The cast and audience waited in a moment of frozen stasis.

Doc smiled vaguely, eyes searching the actors around him.

And walked straight off the other side of the stage, his line undelivered.

Then he'd awakened, sweating.

Ellie had persuaded him to lie down quietly in her own room, pulling off his cracked knee boots herself and bringing him a moistened cloth to lay across his troubled brow.

She had even gone to the trouble of finding her way down into the steaming, noisome kitchen of the Snow Palace, managing to locate some relatively fresh eggs and French poaching them for him. She laid them out on slices of crisp buttered toast and brewed a pot of good coffee.

"And I found this hidden away on the top shelf of one of the closets," she said, delving beneath her loose maroon cloak and triumphantly pulling out a dark green bottle. She drew the cork with a satisfying plopping sound and sniffed at it.

"What is it, my dear?"

"Brandy. Real old, too. Not stuff they brewed up this morning among the junipers on the hillside. I got a couple of glasses as well. Want to try a drink of it? Lift your spirits?"

"Indeed, that would be most gratifying, Ellie. Thank you for your trouble."

"We thesps must stick together, Doc."

"Thesps? Oh, yes, thespians. Members of the acting profession."

"Now, tuck into those eggs, there's a good Theo. Keep your strength up."

"For the performance."

She smiled at him, pouring out a tumbler of the aromatic liqueur. "Need to keep all parts of your performance up, Theo. No good going soft when you need to be hard, is it?"

Doc looked at her, puzzled at the faint stress she seemed to be putting on words like "up" and "parts" and "hard." It baffled him.

But the brandy was delicious, warming him, easing the tension away from his shoulders and relaxing the tightness that gripped his stomach like an overlaced corset.

And the eggs were perfect. The whites firm and the yolks runny.

Ellie had sat on the bottom of the bed, watching him, sipping at her own glass.

"Good?"

"Better than good, my dear. Were it not tautological, I would list all the words I could think of to describe the goodness."

Ellie laid down her glass and stood, moving to the head of the bed at his side. "Lean forward a little, Theo."

"Why?"

"So's I can give you a little massage while you eat your supper."

"Ah, yes. How pleasant."

"Take off your jacket and shirt."

"Should I finish my eggs first?"

"Sure."

Her hands were on his shoulders and neck, pressing gently at the muscles.

"My, but you're like you're made from pieces of spun crystal, Theo."

"I confess that I am a tad nervous about our performance, Ellie." He finished up the last bite of the poached eggs on toast. "Ah, those were magical, my dear."

"Now off with your clothes."

"Just down to my shirt, perhaps?"

She walked over to the door and turned the key in the lock. "There. Now we won't be disturbed. Sorry, I didn't catch your question, Theo?"

To Doc's surprise there suddenly seemed a shortage of oxygen in the bedroom. He was conscious of the smell of his own body, unwashed for too long, of the light scent of the perfumed water that Ellie used, of her frilly underclothes draped neatly over the back of one of the chairs.

And he was stricken with a heart-stopping fear at the realization that he was going to make love with this pretty, frail woman.

"I don't know whether I shall be able..." he began, hardly aware that he'd spoken.

But Ellie wasn't listening. She was busying herself with unlacing her boots, padding to the window to make sure the faded draperies were safely drawn.

Doc started to undress himself, suddenly eager to be naked and under the sheets before she turned around and saw his lined, sagging body. But, to his cautious delight, he discovered that not every part of him was sagging.

The room was lighted by an oil lamp, and Ellie reached over and turned down the wick, using a milled brass wheel. She had taken off everything except her bra and a pair of pink cotton panties.

Just before the light dimmed, Doc noticed how thin the woman was. And there seemed to be small dark patches on her skin. Purplish in color, near her elbow and above her left breast. One planted beneath the prominent ribs.

But they were insignificant.

She bounced into bed, giggling softly, her feet touching Doc's thigh.

"By the Three Kennedys! You're damnably cold, ma'am."

"Sorry, Theo. Guess you'll have to do some warming up."

"The pleasure will be mine," he said, praying inside his head that God would allow him to sustain one of the best erections he'd had in years, what he and his drinking companions at college used to refer to as a regular diamond cutter.

"And you will preserve me from all my wicked enemies?"

He was thrown by that. "I fear that I didn't quite—"

"The play, Theo."

"Oh, of course."

She'd been quoting a line from the middle part of *The Revenge,* when he'd just offered his help to her after Diego had been to her little cottage to threaten her.

"And you will preserve me from all my wicked enemies?" she prompted again.

"Upon my honor, I will."

"That's real good." Her cool fingers tracked across his chest and down. "Oh, Theo... And that's even better!"

In the darkness of the quiet room Doc Tanner smiled to himself.

A memory flash brought back a momentary vision to Doc of the girl called Lori, statuesquely tall and as blond as Kansas wheat; tight blouse, torn, in red satin; her silver-buckled belt; an abbreviated maroon suede skirt; the teetering heels on her crimson boots, glittering spurs with tiny, tinkling bells.

Lori, her face melting as she fell, screaming, into the blazing flames, hands out, clawing toward him in supplication as he watched, helpless. Her hair flaring about her blistered skull. The smoke billowing and closing her off from him forever.

Ellie felt the change in him and stopped moving, reaching around behind and touching him. "Want to rest a moment?"

"No, no. I'll be fine. Just sort of lost it for a moment there. Keep still and then it'll come right on back." Thinking, *Please, let it.*

She laughed, and he felt it as a series of rippling constrictions all around him. "Here you are again, Theo."

Her buttocks were pressed into his lap, bringing a warm and happy memory of making love with his long-lost wife, Emily.

Doc clutched her tight as he came, his head thrown back, tendons straining in his throat. He clapped his own hand over his mouth to muffle his cry of release and pleasure.

Ellie moaned and pushed harder against him, moving her hips faster, until she reached her own climax moments later.

"IF YOU CANNOT help me, sir, then I am lost and needs must give in to his wishes. Satisfy his lusts and let him fuck me."

"No."

"But what can you do for me? It is not my wish

to do this thing and lose my heart and my hope. It is my poverty and not my will consents.''

"I will help you.''

"Will you do anything?''

"Anything.''

He felt her hands pushing him, pressing his head down from her neck, across her breasts, where he nuzzled at her hardened nipples. But now Ellie's fingers were locked into his mane of white hair, forcing him much lower.

"Well, you did say you'd do anything, Theo.'' She giggled.

"The pleasure is all mine.''

"No. Most of it's going to be mine. Then we can see about both having some fun again.''

"Three times!''

"Get to it, Theo.''

Now he was way down the bed, one scrawny leg hanging out in the cold. Ellie's thighs were on either side of his head and he could taste her body, salt on his tongue.

He was going to try to remember another line from the play to amuse her, but he recalled his own mother always insisting it was terribly bad manners to speak with your mouth full.

Doc woke in Ellie's bed, feeling tired, finding that his chest and shoulders were a mass of bites and scratches.

Apart from that he felt better than he had in many long months.

Maybe years.

Ellie was missing and he got up, washing himself quickly in the bowl of cold water, using a rough blue towel to dry his face and body.

Outside the window he could see that the gray skies had vanished and it looked blue from north to south. And it didn't seem to be so cold.

The door opened and he swung around, seeing Ryan Cawdor grinning at him.

"What's so damned funny that you have to stand there like a Barbary ape, Cawdor?"

"I was smiling at the smile on your face, Doc. That's all. Like a cat that got the best of the cream, if you know what I mean."

"What do you want?" Doc asked, fighting to control his grin and failing.

Ryan leaned a hand against the wall. "Thought you might like to know. Rosie just gave us the word that Sidler's better. You go on tonight."

Chapter Thirty-Three

Capestrano called a last rehearsal for the middle of the afternoon, insisting that they needed to check out the technical aspects of the night's performance, particularly the use of the rear exit for the melodramatic climax of the plot.

J.B. stayed behind in the boarding house while Ryan sat out front and watched the final run-through of the play.

The weather outside was idyllic. There had been a heaven of a sunrise, and a golden sun soared across the snow-crusted Rockies. The temperature had risen several degrees above freezing, and water was running and gurgling in the gutters of the houses, melting in the streets and alleys.

Several of the sec men had come into the Multiplex, lounging near the back, their slush-stained boots resting on seats.

Three of the five killers also appeared during the rehearsals: Twenty Gooseneck, his veiled eyes seeming to see nothing and everything; Julio, flash-ily dressed, toying with his Texas Longhorn Bor-

der Special revolver. The lights from the stage
dancing off the pale blue silk of his tight-fitting
shirt.

And Reena Miller, her black leather jacket un-
buttoned, showing the Colt Cobra .38 in its shoulder holster. She sat near the front, two rows behind
Ryan, watching in silence.

He turned around, deliberately staring at her, not
wanting the woman to psych him out by her presence. Her gold-and-silver eyes looked back at him,
betraying no emotion.

"Want to sit here?" he said.

"Sure. Like I want to suck a dead cougar's dick,
One-eye."

Ryan smiled. "Fuck you, too, lady."

CAPESTRANO HELD UP A HAND. "And this is where
we shall invite five members of the audience to
come onstage to represent the evil band. They will
be taken out the back, through the passage to the
rear door. Ryan, perhaps you and J.B. might help
to conduct them? Good. Then they can come
around front to relish the final curtain and join in
the turbulent waves of applause that will fill the
auditorium."

The rehearsal had gone well. Ryan had both seen
and heard all of the play several times since their
arrival in Yuma, but to see it actually working,

with everyone in costume, made a difference that came close to being magical.

Before the performance they all went back to the Snow Palace. And there, over a reasonable fish stew, Ryan gathered everyone around and told them, in a low voice, about his plan.

"Figure that Jennison and the others are going to stick together. Probably come when Sidler comes to see the play."

"But we don't know when that'll be," Ellie interrupted.

"True."

"Don't even know if he's coming at all," J.B. added.

"True again," Ryan said patiently. "But we know that the chances of lifting the baron himself are remote. But it should be just that little bit easier to get the boy's killers."

"And that is all you need to rescue your own son and friends from the embrace of the Baron Nelson of Vista?" Capestrano nodded. "But how will you capture them from the heart of this pesthole without all of us becoming buzzard feed?"

Ellie whooped out loud. "I know!" She instantly dropped her head penitently, index finger sealing her lips. "Forgive me," she said, in an exaggerated stage whisper. "I'll be quiet and very discreet. But I have just seen what you intend, Ryan."

"What?" he asked, mildly irritated that the washed-out blond woman might have guessed what he'd been planning for the past couple of days.

"The end of the play. Bring Jennison up and the others."

"Yeah. If they'll come. That's your bit, Ellie."

She smiled and blew him a kiss. "I can charm birds from trees and butterflies from the nectared heart of the cowslip."

Doc smiled at her, his head to one side. "I can vouch for that, my dear Ryan. Indeed I can. The lady has charms to soothe even the most savage of breasts."

Capestrano picked at a ragged piece of skin around his thumbnail. "It'll be..." He hesitated. "Dangerous, won't it, Ryan?"

"Sure. But we'll do everything we can to make sure we all get through."

"Who will subdue these sons of bitches?" Ellie asked.

"J.B. gets the rig and steals another horse. Waits in the alley once we know that Sidler and the others are there. With our mounts as well. I'm close by. Club them down."

Michael cleared his throat. "How do we all get out? We'll still be on stage."

"Take the curtain call," Ryan explained. "Nobody'll suspect anything wrong. Think it's part of the play. Then you all come out the same way to the alley, and we head south as fast as we can go. Chances are most of the audience is going to head for the nearest bar or gaudy and start drinking right off."

Ellie turned to Diego. "We could arrange that they are taken through one at a time."

"How?"

"Say there is a frail bridge to the hiding place that will only carry the weight of two people at a time. That will mean Ryan and John can capture them more easily."

"Yeah," Ryan said. "Might work if that could be done."

Capestrano considered the question for several seconds. "Why not?" he said slowly. "Yes, why not try that?"

Knuckles had been helping himself to a third portion of the fish stew, though by now it had congealed into a wizened crust around the edges with a film of rainbow grease floating at its center.

"How do we know if Sidler comes tonight?"

Ryan stood. "I'll go and see what I can find out.

The Owen woman says there's a big buzz around the ville about the play.''

"Hope they don't start shooting.'' Ellie sighed. "Hate it if they start opening up with blasters. Place fills with smoke and you can't see halfway across the stage.''

IT WAS STILL MILD as Ryan hurried back from the Multiplex toward the Snow Palace, with the first stars appearing against the darkening evening sky.

He raced through the deserted lobby, up the creaking stairs and into the main bedroom.

"It's on,'' he said. "Sec men outside reckon Sidler's coming tonight.''

THE PLAY WENT WELL. Everybody turned up more or less on time, cast and audience.

Nobody forgot their lines.

Nobody bumped into the furniture.

The Multiplex was crowded with men and women, and even a few children. They laughed and cheered in all of the right places and stood and stamped their approval at the play's climax.

Twenty Gooseneck wasn't there.

Reena Miller wasn't there.

Ossie Grant and Julio weren't there.

Nor was Jim Jennison.

Baron Wizard Sidler sent word that he still

wasn't feeling too well, and he was sorry but he wouldn't be coming to the performance.

Maybe the next night.

"MEBBE NEXT NIGHT," J.B. said, pulling off his combat boots and swinging his feet onto his bed.

"Be the night of the eighth day." Ryan bit his lip, fighting away the tension.

The two old friends were alone in their room. The others were all with Capestrano in his room along the corridor, enjoying their success over a bottle of tart, fizzy wine that Ellie had bought from Rosie Owen.

"Have to be tomorrow. No choice, J.B., is there? Tomorrow."

Chapter Thirty-Four

The dowager baroness of Vista ville sat in a deep winged armchair, the brocade torn across the back, holding a small chromed pistol in her birdlike hand. Her long white hair poured over her shoulders like a frozen fall of fresh snow.

Her eyes were wide, the pale blue swamped by the drugged circles of the pupils.

"Just do it easy, bitch," she said very quietly.

Krysty waited behind a diamond-shaped table, its top inlaid with a variety of wooden veneers. An unusual vase of yellow-and-cream glass stood at the center, holding some dried rushes. Mildred was close to the door, one hand resting on Dean's shoulder.

They'd been brought to the old woman's chambers by Rick Coburn.

It was late evening on the seventh day since Ryan, J.B., Doc and Michael had left the ville for the trail north.

The sec boss had been uneasy, unwilling to talk

as he led them through the paneled corridors of the fortress.

"Why does she want to see us?" Krysty had asked. "Why not the baron?"

"Can't say."

"You mean you won't say." Mildred shook her head. "That makes it into bad news."

He stopped. "I'm not sure. But I said I wouldn't lie to you, and I won't. Better Ryan gets back here with prisoners."

"Or what?" Dean asked.

"Old lady was broken up by Zebe's murder and by Clare dying the way she did. I don't really know the rights or the wrongs of it. But she pushed the baron harder and harder."

"Still doesn't answer why she'd want to see us all now."

Coburn hesitated. "Been drinking, doing some serious downers. Think it's mainly you, Krysty... mainly you she wants."

The old woman was wearing what looked like the shredded remnants of an antique wedding dress, cream silk, faded past ivory toward yellow, the lace so fragile that it resembled the bundled webs of a hundred spiders.

"You don't do it easy, then you'll end doing it fucking hard."

"That all you wanted to say?"

"Show some respect, you flame-haired slag!"

"Baron said he wanted me to be his son," Dean said. "Me."

There was a bright laugh from the dowager, a laugh that sounded like warm blood spraying onto cold stainless steel.

"Sure, sonny. You'll keep Alferd happy until something better comes along. That something being his own flesh from the dry slits of these whores."

"Prince among men, your son, lady." Mildred looked at Krysty. "Why don't we just leave her to her sick fancies?"

"You don't understand, do you?" There was a strange hiss in the woman's voice, like the November wind blowing between the shingles on the broken roof of an abandoned church.

"Nothing to understand." Krysty shook her head pityingly. "Gaia! You don't see that the way out of this tragedy is to look forward. Let your son find another woman he can love. Love, not fuck. And then he can have another child and struggle back to something like normal. But not this way."

It was as though she hadn't spoken a single word.

The only sound was the pine wood crackling in the fireplace. The wind had veered and occasional wraiths of smoke came floating out into the room.

The thick walls of the old hotel kept any other sounds far at bay.

"There are chains, redhead. Chains for the black bitch and for the brat-child if he rebels against his new father. We can have sec men break your knees and elbows and wrists and fingers and toes and shoulders and jaw." She laughed again, with a flat, crazy sound. "None of those parts matter to us. It's your wombs we need, and we can take them. Even if we have your arms and legs hacked off your body."

"Oh, Christ!" Mildred turned away. "You make me want to throw up, lady. Sooner the Good Lord takes you to Him, the better and cleaner this world's going to be."

The gun barked once.

It was only a purse blaster, a .22 caliber. But the dowager baroness was using cross-filled bullets that expanded like mushrooms when they impacted with their target.

Mildred felt the warm breath of the lead as it missed her face by inches and smashed into the wall of the room, digging a spray of plaster out a hole the size of a man's fist.

"Watch your mouth, you frigid witch-bitch."

Nobody moved. Dean's hand was on the turquoise hilt of his favored knife, but Mildred's hand was on his arm, holding him in check.

"Your son gave his oath," Krysty said. "Ryan comes back in two days with the men the baron wants and we all go free."

Mildred was watching the old woman's eyes and she breathed out a quiet "Oh."

The barrel of the pistol was drilling between her breasts. "What is it?"

Krysty echoed the dowager's question. "Yeah, what is it?"

"You don't feel it?"

"Feel?" Krysty closed her emerald-bright eyes for a moment, brow wrinkling with concentration. "Oh, Mildred."

"You two wise women, or something?" the baron's mother asked, her voice scraping up the scale. "Answer me or I'll chill you both. Might chill you both anyways if you're fucking witches."

"Then Alferd doesn't get himself a new son and heir, does he?" Mildred spat.

Krysty's face was slack with shock. "I never saw it. How could I have been so triple-stupe to have missed it?"

"What?"

"Course. He's not going to keep his word. That was all shit. If Ryan doesn't come back, he uses us like brood mares and takes Dean as his own. Chills us once we've given him children." She shuddered as though seized by an ague. "And if

Ryan does keep his part, the freak bastard mutie has him killed anyway.''

"Ryan'll butcher him," Dean protested, his eyes narrowed in anger at the betrayal.

"Words are cheap, little man," the old woman sneered. "Think the sec men would allow anyone close enough to Alferd?''

Mildred remembered the mercenaries who'd ridden in from Yuma. "Six mercies took out the little boy, easy as snuffing a candle. You think men like Ryan Cawdor and John Dix would let treachery pass unpunished?''

The dowager shrugged, the gun still pointed at the black woman. "Don't care.''

Dean pushed Mildred away from him, drawing his blade from its sheath, advancing toward the white-haired dowager.

"No," Krysty warned, also moving in the direction of the woman in the chair.

"Dad would want me to zero her," the boy said, switching the knife from hand to hand, like a magician preparing a trick.

"I won't kill you, child.''

"No. But I'll kill you.''

He was less than ten short strides away from her. The click of the hammer of the revolver being thumbed back was surprisingly loud.

"I'll put one through your leg. Cripple you and

that'll be a shame. Stop you going running and hunting with your father.''

Dean stood still. He'd seen what the .22 had done to a solid wall, and he had more than enough imagination and experience to visualize what the bullet would do to his leg.

"Krysty?" Mildred said.

"Yeah," she replied, picking up instantly on the mental shorthand. "We have to do it soon."

"Now?"

Krysty nodded. "Why not?"

Dean looked at the two women, struggling to hang on to what was going on, puzzled.

The dowager shook her head in malignant irritation, the gesture making her long hair fall like a curtain over her eyes.

Outside the room, though none of them was aware of it, there was the sound of heavy boots mounting the staircase.

"Now," Krysty said.

She dived quickly to her right, the sudden movement attracting the attention of the old woman, the barrel of the little revolver swinging toward her.

But Mildred also made her play, dodging and crouching to her left, splitting the dowager's attention. The gun wavered.

Dean had the fastest reflexes, and he dropped to

his knees and started to crawl toward the chair, knife in his teeth.

The blaster cracked twice, and someone screamed.

The door was thrown open and the towering figure of Baron Nelson strode in, to be confronted by his mother, holding out bloodstained hands.

"I'm sorry, son," she whispered.

Chapter Thirty-Five

The performance on the previous night had seemed to Ryan to be superbly successful. But both Diego and Ellie had a variety of comments and criticisms, calling everyone together for a discussion after a late breakfast, which was served by a Rose Owen who was starry-eyed with delight from her enjoyment of the play.

"You was fuckin' wonderful, all of you. Liked the bit where you all got to fuck together. Good that was."

They hadn't finished eating when they heard feet clattering along the corridor toward their large bedroom.

"Sec men," J.B. warned, rolling off his bed and grabbing the Smith & Wesson M-4000 12-gauge scattergun, loaded with the fléchettes.

"Not in here," Ryan said urgently. "Not a firefight in here."

J.B. knelt behind the bed, out of sight of anyone coming in, holding the lethal shotgun at the ready.

Without even the minimal courtesy of a knock,

the door was flung open and in trooped half a dozen of the ville's finest, a ragged, vicious crew, unshaved and scruffy.

Their leader was one of the guards on the barrier on the blacktop into Yuma.

"Told to tell you Baron Sidler's coming tonight. For definite."

Ryan noticed that Ossie Grant was there again, hanging around at the back of the group, bicolored eyes darting everywhere.

"Thanks. Be ready at eight to give him a real good show."

"Liked it last night," said one of the men, unable to stop boggling at Ellie, who was lying on the sofa, wearing a thin cotton robe that revealed more of her thighs than it hid.

She smiled at him, got up, taking care to show just a little bit more of herself, and kissed the man on the cheeks. "Bless you, my dear sweet man," she whispered. "Bless you all."

"I liked it, too," a second man complained.

But the leader of the group punched him on the arm. "Just shut your mouth!"

He turned to Ryan. "That's the message, all right?"

"He and his friends coming to the play tonight?" Ryan asked, pointing at Ossie Grant, who was already halfway out of the door.

"Yeah. Baron comes, then they come. Specially that Reena." He laughed and nudged the sec man next to him.

Ossie Grant glowered at Ryan. "One of your group not here. Word is there's another. Little bastard in glasses."

"Yeah. At the stable."

They left the room, and everyone waited until the sound of their boots had faded away into the morning stillness.

Capestrano whistled between his teeth. "Rather play a hundred years of romantic slush than go through that ghastly moment again. I felt as though I had a big sign flashing upon my forehead. 'This man is going to kidnap your baron.' Know what I mean? And what is all this about John Dix? I can only assume, my friends, that there must be a small something that you haven't told us."

Ryan looked at the Armorer, who'd scrambled up onto his bed, tipping back his fedora. "What I know, Diego, you know."

J.B. WRAPPED HIMSELF UP against the cool wind that had returned from the north, going out alone in the late morning and returning after they'd finished eating the rabbit and jalapeño stew.

He sat and ladled a plateful for himself, dipping

in his spoon, tasting it. "Hey, that's not bad. Got some bite to it."

"I helped her cook it," Ellie said. "Threw out the meat she was going to serve us. Could've been horse, but it had a kind of layer of green fur to it, so it was hard to tell."

"Where have you been, John?" Knuckles asked, his finger stroking the rad scar on his face.

"Around the place. Checked the stable again. Thought I best make sure they had the same horses in there. Throw the plan off center if I got there tonight and found there wasn't enough animals to draw the wag out of the alley."

Ryan glanced across the table at his old friend, knowing that J.B. was lying. No, not exactly lying. But not exactly telling the truth, either.

Not the whole truth.

There was something about his whole body language that made Ryan suspect that the Armorer had finally got the information he'd been waiting for. Ever since they first came to Yuma.

AFTER THE MEAL had been cleared away, Monsignor Diego Capestrano lived up to his image of being a stern taskmaster, insisting that they must all go down to the Multiplex and rehearse yet again, ready for the evening.

"Particularly the scene where the villains are

tricked into going out the back alley,'' he said. ''That most specially.''

''I'll stay here.'' J.B. caught Ryan's eye. ''You going?''

''No.''

THEY STOOD TOGETHER by the window, watching as the rest of the group walked along the muddied street, down through the sunlit ville toward Sidler's headquarters.

''I like them,'' J.B. said.

''Me, too. That boy Knuckles got a real tilted load to carry all his days. He does well.''

''You think Ellie's got some kind of an illness, Ryan?''

''Yeah. You see it?''

''Rad sickness.''

Ryan nodded. ''That's my guess. Far on. Real cruel shame.''

''Nobody ever said that life was going to be fair, did they?''

''No.''

''You worried about them not making it all the way across when we make the draw tonight?''

J.B. didn't answer at first, contenting himself with rubbing an index finger over the condensation that lined the inside of the window.

Ryan repeated the question. "You think there'll be blood in the dirt?"

"Think it's likely."

"Good plan."

"Sure. Never knew you come up with a bad plan, Ryan. Not in all the years we walked in each other's shadows."

"But?"

The Armorer swung away and walked to sit on the sofa. "But there's likely to be blood spilled in the dirt."

"Capestrano or Ellie or Knuckles? They're most likely to buy the farm."

"Sure. But bullets don't know if you're clever at firefights, do they?"

"Course not. Trader used to say that a full-metal jacket had an awful lot of power and damned little brains."

"We got no choice, have we, Ryan? Less we go back and try and rescue Mildred, Krysty and the boy. Dark night! That's a more dangerous option than the one we got here."

"What did you want to tell me, J.B.? Just that you weren't happy with what was going down here? Is that all?"

"No."

Ryan sat at the table. "Because I'm not happy about it, either."

"It's not that!" The Armorer raised his voice, flecks of high color darkening his usually sallow cheeks.

"Then what?"

Somewhere in the depths of the boarding house they heard a door slam and several voices raised in anger. Then another door closed and the voices were silenced.

"It's like you said, Ryan."

"About this ville?"

"About the people in it. Well, just one person in it."

"Wizard Sidler?"

"No. Not him."

"The five killers?"

J.B. shook his head, eyes closed. "This is a seriously bad scene, friend."

"You know one of them? The woman! Not your wife, is she?"

"No. That'd be an easy one. It's not her, Ryan. No, that'd be easy."

"Which man?" Then he had a strong feeling, remembering in his mind's eye what they all looked like. "Jennison?"

"Yeah."

"What about him?"

"Jim Jennison and me are kin, Ryan. We got the same father. He's my half brother." He paused. "There. Now you know it."

Chapter Thirty-Six

Ryan stood at the side of the stage, looking out into the auditorium, watching the faces of the audience that filled the dusty plush seats.

Wizard Sidler, Baron of Yuma, was in the front row, still wearing the black clothes that made him look like the bald shootist in the film about the seven gunmen who'd gone to shoo some flies from a village in Mexico.

Reena Miller was sitting on his left, her right hand busy in the dark shadows that clustered in his lap.

Twenty Gooseneck was next along the line from the woman. Ossie Grant and Julio sat immediately behind the baron.

At first Ryan couldn't see Jim Jennison. Then there was movement at the back, a swirl among the crowd, like mackerel when a shark was passing close by. The pale, short gunman picked his way slowly down the aisle, taking the one empty seat immediately to the right of Wizard Sidler.

Though Jennison was physically unimpressive,

like J.B., his half brother, he had much the same sort of strength of presence, the kind of man you looked at once and ignored. Then you looked a second time and you were quick to step aside.

J.B. was at the livery stable, ostensibly checking out the rig and their horses, actually getting ready to make his move as soon as Ryan came and gave him the word.

They'd timed the play at both the dress rehearsal and the previous night's performance. It ran eighty-five minutes, without the intermission. The key scene where the desperadoes were lured from the audience came after seventy-five minutes.

Capestrano appeared silently at Ryan's elbow, peering around the moth-eaten curtain. "Good house," he said approvingly.

"And we got the special guests we wanted. Everything okay backstage?"

"Surely." He turned away, stopped and looked back at Ryan, holding out his hand. "Just like to say, in case we don't get another opportunity, Ryan, that it has been a pleasure to know you and your friends. A great pleasure."

"Sorry we sucked you into this, Diego. Not your fight."

The chubby little man smiled. "We do an entertainment that we call *Saddle-saws,* using quotes from the great actors of the old Western vids. One of them says—'' he hunched his shoulders and adopted a hoarse voice ''—'There's some things that a man can't ride around.' Like that. Well, this is one of those things that a man isn't able to ride around. You understand that, Ryan?''

"Yeah, I do. And I'm glad to shake your hand, Diego. And the hands of Knuckles and Ellie."

Capestrano looked around. "I think that Mistress Morte has been shaking more than just the hand of the excellent Dr. Tanner." And he chuckled. "Now, the world's a stage and I must go and strut and fret for an hour or so. Until later."

He clasped Ryan's hand in a surprisingly firm, dry grip.

"IF YOU CANNOT HELP ME, sir, then I am lost and needs must give in to his wishes. Satisfy his lusts and let him fuck me."

"I'll fuck you, darling!" bellowed a voice from near the back of the theater.

"No," Doc said, stamping his silver-topped cane on the stage and glaring angrily out into the darkness.

Ellie shook her head and sobbed. "But what can you do for me? It is not my wish to do this thing and lose my heart and my hope. It is my poverty and not my will consents."

She fell weeping to her knees, silencing the

rowdy audience. Doc moved to stand by her, putting a hand on her shoulder, raising his sword stick in a defensive way.

"Go to it, old man!" someone called.

Ryan glanced at his wrist chron. The play had been running now for just over the hour. It was going well. Sidler had been seen to laugh and applaud several times, once leaping to his feet and putting a bullet from one of his matched Navy Colts into the ceiling, showering the front three rows with a white cloud of plaster.

It was time to go around the rear of the stage into the maze of little passages and darkened rooms, to the exit door with its bar lock.

Time to go and warn J.B. that the deal was going down.

THE CINEMA WAS WARM and smoke-filled, the area out the back cooler and fresher.

When Ryan opened the door, propping it with a wooden wedge, it was about nine o'clock. There was a bright moon, gleaming silver off the patches of slick ice in the alley. The temperature was around ten degrees below freezing, and a light wind blew from the east.

It was good weather for making a fast escape from a ville.

Good weather for anyone organizing a pursuit.

HE WAS BACK at the side of the stage. A few moments earlier Ryan had caught the faint sound of a horse snickering, and he wondered whether Sidler was careful enough to post sentries around the old cinema. He decided from everything they'd seen, that he wasn't that sort of baron.

Ellie had just stepped to the front of the stage, dropping a deep curtsy to the audience, somehow contriving to aim her charm specifically at Wizard Sidler.

"My lords and ladies," she began, waiting with a patient smile until the whooping and the whistling had faded away.

Sidler slowly stood, allowing his narrowed eyes to scan the rows of seats. His hands hovered over the grips of the antique revolvers and Ryan, spying around the curtain, realized he was modeling his pose on gunfighters in vids.

"Let the little lady say what she has to," he growled, spitting on the carpet and nodding at the immediate silence that followed his order. "Young stupes now...all gall and no sand." He bowed to Ellie. "On you go, my dear."

"Thank you kindly, Baron. I'm much obliged to you for that."

"Get on with it," Ryan whispered. Every minute that passed generated a greater risk of someone wandering past the alley and seeing J.B. with the wagon and the spare horses.

"For this part of the play we need six people to portray the gang of lawless villains that are being hired to kidnap me and butcher my true and loyal friends. You will come to no harm and will be returned to your seats in time to witness the climactic moments of our play."

"I done it last night." The voice came from the far right.

Ellie blew the voice a kiss. "And very good he was, too."

Sidler stood. "I wanna be one of the outlaw gang," he bellowed, slapping himself on the chest. "How about that?"

Ryan smiled to himself. The man was such a stupe it was hard to think of him as being behind the cruel torture and slaughter of a little boy. But he knew that the truly wicked could easily look like evangelical priests on vacation.

Ellie didn't miss a beat. "How about the lovely lady at your side, Baron? She care to pretend to be wicked for a few minutes?"

Reena Miller uncoiled from her seat, brushing back the cascade of raven hair. "I'll be wicked when I fucking like, lady."

"There's two. Four more." She held out her

hands to Jennison, Gooseneck, Julio and Ossie Grant. "You, perhaps?"

Led by Sidler, the killers filed dutifully onto the stage, looking embarrassed at the wave of applause that Ellie generated for them.

Ryan vanished from the side of the stage, ready for the last act.

The famous final scene.

Chapter Thirty-Seven

There was a dark space, just inside the rear entrance to the Multiplex. Outside there was the silver rectangle of moonlight and the dull glitter of the ice.

Ryan and J.B. couldn't hope to conceal the sound of the horses and the burro, hooves clacking, harness jingling. The hope was that it would all be done so quickly none of the killers would have any time to consider there was something wrong.

They waited in the blackness, ready for Ellie to bring them the first of the gang.

They heard her giggling, and the slap of a hand. "Oh, Baron, that's naughty of you."

"I'm supposed to be a sexed-up outlaw, so that's what I am. How about a quick blowjob here and now, Ellie?"

"Spoil the play, Baron. But tell you what. I'll come to your rooms right after the last act's over. I'll start by sucking hard, and it'll just get harder and harder. That be good?"

"Hell, sounds better than good. After you, little lady."

"No, you know the way better than me, Baron. You go first."

Ryan saw the figure, silhouetted perfectly against the moonlight. He and J.B. had rehearsed the attacks in the bedroom.

He stepped in and swung both fists at the man's kidneys, while J.B. used the butt of the Smith & Wesson to crack the stumbling baron across the side of the skull.

Sidler went down with nothing louder than a muffled grunt that could have been shock or pain.

There was no talk between Ryan and J.B. as they heaved the unconscious man into the bed of the rig. The Armorer had liberated some baling wire from the stable and cut it into short lengths. He tugged Sidler's arms behind him and looped the wire around his wrists, twisting it tight.

Ellie had stood there for a moment, as though she'd been struck by lightning, her hands to her mouth. Ryan turned to her.

"Great. One down. Five to go. You're doing terrific, Ellie." He stooped to kiss the trembling woman quickly on her cold cheek and pushed her gently back toward the stage.

Gooseneck, the mutie, was the second victim.

As they lifted him into the wagon, blood was trickling from his mouth, nose and ears.

"Nelson won't pay us for no cold meat," Ryan said.

Ossie Grant was third in line. He half turned from Ryan, sensing a trap, and J.B. had to coldcock him with the butt of the shotgun, hitting him in the throat while Ryan stepped silently in and took him from the side.

The Armorer knelt again with a fresh strip of the baling wire. "We got the minimum we need to save Mildred, Krysty and Dean," he said, panting a little with the effort of lifting the unconscious bodies into the back of the wagon.

"Reckon we should just chill the other three?" Ryan asked.

"Quick and safe."

"Might lose one or two on the road."

J.B. nodded, glasses flashing in the moonlight.

"Guess so. Heads up, Ryan. Got us another customer coming."

Julio went down like a lamb.

"Audience is getting restive," Ellie warned. "Want to go through on the last pair?"

Ryan nodded. "Ville without these five killers and without their baron's going to be like a headless chicken."

"Give us more time to make it away," J.B. agreed.

Reena Miller nearly got clear. She must have suspected something was wrong, because she already had her .38 Colt Cobra drawn in her hand, pushing Ellie ahead of her through the dark passages toward the door.

Ryan chopped at her wrist with the edge of his palm, the pistol rattling on the concrete. Reena yelped and tried to spin and kick at him, but J.B. was on the other side, swinging the Smith & Wesson into the pit of her stomach. She dropped to her knees, puking and gasping for breath. Ryan didn't hesitate, kicking her in the side of the head.

"Tough bitch," J.B. said conversationally, busy with the wire.

"She's a woman…" Ellie's voice trembled with barely contained shock.

"She's a coldheart bitch," Ryan replied. "Start feeling sorry for someone like Reena Miller and you find yourself on your back with the rain falling in your open eyes."

"There's only that one, Jennison, left. Do I have to…"

"Yeah. Do it. Then get on with the last part of the plan."

Ellie came to hold him for support, but he pushed her away. There wasn't time for that.

J.B. glanced at his chron. "Running late, Ryan."

"Five down. Only one more for us to take. Jim Jennison."

The Armorer gave him a half smile. "Just one to take," he repeated.

In the rig, one of their victims was recovering consciousness, starting to moan. Ryan hopped quickly in and found it was Julio. The blond hair was clotted with dark blood, and the pale blue eyes were open and staring.

"Gimme a..." he began.

Ryan slipped the SIG-Sauer from its holster and clubbed him behind the ear.

"Back to sleep," he said.

He and J.B. waited for Ellie to return for the last time.

They could hear the heels of her lace-up boots clacking on the stone, drowning out the sound of anyone accompanying her.

The feet stopped, just at the opening to the last room before the exit.

There was a silence, for thirty heartbeats. Ryan looked over at J.B., who shrugged, holding up the scattergun to indicate his suspicion that something was wrong.

"You there, brother?" Nobody spoke. Jennison's voice called again. "John Dix?"

There was no point in maintaining silence. If Jennison knew, then the only possible hope was for them to try to close him down quickly.

If it wasn't already too late for that.

"What is it, Jim?"

"Figure you and that one-eyed motherfucker got Sidler and the others." It wasn't a question. "Well, I got me the little lady here. Got the blade about one breath away from opening her throat."

Ryan spoke. "We got most of what we came for. Let Ellie go and we'll let you walk away free, Jennison."

"Sounds like the sort of deal a man might try for when he's holding a pair of deuces and he knows the man across the table's got at least three kings. Only a matter of time before these ragged lamebrain sec bastards realize you picked out their beloved fucking leader. Then goodbye will be all she wrote for you, my brother and everyone."

"Half brother. Your mother fucked my father once. Long years ago. The night he got you, his mind was someplace else."

Jennison laughed. "Same old J. B. Dix. I'd heard you was dead, brother. Somewhere up in the Darks, couple of years ago. Along with that sheepfucker, the Trader."

Ryan couldn't see a play. If there was a chance to get Jennison, even if it meant Ellie buying the farm, he'd have taken it. Tough, but that was the way it was. But it was a Colorado standoff, with the dice favoring Jennison.

"Then I heard Trader might still be this side of the dark river. Figured that could mean my older brother was also up and walking good."

"You heard right."

"Nelson sent you." Again, there was no suggestion of it being a question. "His stinking, shitting, loudmouthed little prick of a son. Bastard had it all coming."

J.B. answered him. "Doesn't matter who's right or wrong, Jennison."

"Just who's left behind, brother."

The killer was playing for time against Ryan and J.B.

And he was winning.

"You got Ellie with you?"

"Sure, One-Eye. Ryan Cawdor. There's another name I heard plenty around Deathlands. Where there's shit, there's Cawdor."

The voice was inching closer. Ryan was sure of it. And his keen hearing had caught the faint sound of heels dragging on the dusty stone. Jennison was hauling Ellie with him, keeping her quiet with the threat of the knife at her neck.

The options had narrowed down to one.

Open fire into the blackness with the SIG-Sauer.

A few of the fifteen rounds might hit Jennison. But it definitely meant Ellie's death, one way or the other.

As Ryan tightened his finger on the trigger of the blaster, he heard the dull sound of wood striking against bone.

Honed metal on stone.

A gasp that was almost a scream came from Ellie.

And a nervous laugh came from Knuckles. "Me thought that bastard had seen through our trick. So me followed him here."

"He's laid Jennison out cold," Ellie said. "Quick, before he recovers."

J.B. moved in, calling back to Ryan. "Got a lump on the side of his skull the size of a vulture's egg. But he's breathing."

"Knuckles. You did great." Ryan glanced out into the alley, but there was nobody in sight. "Get back with Ellie. Wrap the play up, and then come out here as fast as you can. Just like we all planned it."

"Will we be all right?" Ellie was gripping Ryan's hand like a drowning woman.

"Sure. All downhill from here."

Chapter Thirty-Eight

Capestrano sat on the buckboard seat of the wag, with Knuckles beside him, managing the two-horse team. Ellie was in the back, under the hastily drawn canvas hood, in charge of the captured weapons and the bound prisoners. Ryan had given her a length of four-by-two and told her not to hesitate to use it.

"Any of them look like they're coming around, whack them behind the ear."

"Be a pleasure. Specially that son of a bitch Jennison. Oh, sorry, John. Forgot he was your half brother."

"Yeah, but son of a bitch'll do. My father, but not my mother, Ellie."

Ryan led the way on his amiable, surefooted skewbald. Doc came second on the towering black stallion, his Le Mat stuck in his belt, head bowed against the cold wind. The wag was in the middle of the group with a packhorse tethered to the tail. Michael complained endlessly on the ridge-backed burro. "Why couldn't you have stolen me a real

horse, J.B.? I just started to get my blisters healed
and now I'll have them all over again.''

The Armorer was rearguard on his trim little bay
mare, the Uzi held loosely in his right hand, constantly turning around to look behind them for any
sign of pursuers.

They'd made their getaway from the Multiplex
in excellent time. The play had finished to riotous
applause, and nobody there had seemed to be taking all that much notice of the missing baron and
his five hired killers.

But Ryan knew that it was only a matter of time
before someone started wondering where the six
people had gone, would find there was a horse
missing from the stable and that the Snow Palace
had suddenly lost seven of its paying guests.

Now they were approaching the barrier across
the one narrow blacktop running in and out of the
ville of Yuma.

The bright moon was still riding high above the
rockies all around them, but it was now thinly
veiled behind ragged shreds of cloud, like the cloak
of a beggar.

It was just a few minutes short of ten o'clock,
but Ryan didn't expect the guards to be particularly
alert.

Only one of them was out in the open, with two
more standing in the doorway of the little hut. The

sec man held a carbine in his hands, pointing at the ground, showing he didn't anticipate any trouble.

Like the other details of their plan, Ryan and J.B. were ready for more or less anything that might happen.

"Hey there!"

On the way into Yuma Ryan had spotted a thin pair of wires running from the roof of the hut toward the ville. Obviously some kind of walkie, probably linked to the Multiplex.

"Yo," Ryan called. "Monsignor Diego Capestrano and his theater company, leaving the ville." He reined in the horse, holding up a hand to stop the rig behind him.

"Saw your play last night. You got the little lady on board there?"

Ellie poked her head between the shoulders of Knuckles and Diego, blowing the man a kiss. "I am here, and I remember seeing you in the audience. Thank you for your applause."

"We was there, too," said one of the guards in the doorway.

"And my love to you as well," the woman trilled. "I'll maybe see you all when next we play Yuma. That would be thrilling."

All three sec men stared up at her, as though she

were a goddess paying a fleeting visit to Earth. Ryan coughed.

"Could you heft the barrier and we'll be on our way?"

"Baron given you clearance?"

"Of course."

"How come we haven't been told?"

Ryan felt the faint prickle of impending action, careful not to move his hand toward the butt of the blaster.

Not yet.

Ellie spoke again. "Dear Wizard was in the front row tonight. He so enjoyed it. Positively ordered us to return in a month or so to perform a different play for him."

The guard at the barrier nodded and tipped it up, the counterbalanced end rising in a gentle arc. "Sure, lady. There you go."

Ryan waved the small convoy onward. "Obliged," he said.

"NOT TOO FAST." He stood in the stirrups and stared back toward the distant lights of the pesthole ville. But there was no sign of any pursuit. The trio of sec men had retreated into their hut, and the barrier was down again across the blacktop.

The wind had dropped to nothing, and the night was infinitely still and quiet.

They had traveled at least a mile down the winding highway when Ryan's keen hearing caught the faint sound of a bell, a tinny noise that rang for about ten seconds before it stopped.

"Alarm message to the sec men," he called to the others. "Can of worms got opened. Let's go!"

Like many frontier villes, Yuma hadn't contained many gas wags. In fact, Ryan had only seen a couple. One was a flatbed truck with the rear wheels missing, the other a rusting old auto wag located at the rear of the livery stable. He'd taken the extra precaution of ripping out a handful of wires from its engine, just in case.

If they could get a decent running start, he reckoned that they should have a fair chance of holding off any pursuers on horseback. That was one of the reasons that he'd doubled up the team for the rig.

Ryan figured that the biggest plus they had on their side was that the ville would be in some chaos. And from what he'd seen of other villes when a baron disappeared or was killed, there wasn't always that enthusiastic a movement to try to rescue or replace him.

JUST BEFORE MIDNIGHT the sky clouded and the temperature dropped. A few flurries of fresh snow began to sprinkle the trail south.

Since Ryan had the rifle, he and J.B. changed

roles. The Armorer took up point, leading the way carefully through the dark woods, along the valleys, climbing up the flanks of the mountain.

And he deliberately fell behind, pausing at every vantage point, checking for any sign of pursuit from Yuma.

It was just after one in the morning when Ryan spotted horsemen, coming along the trail in a group. He counted eight of them.

The one-eyed man swung out of the saddle and looped the horse's bridle around the broken branch of a stunted alder.

Pressing the smooth walnut stock of the SSG-70 Steyr bolt-action rifle against his shoulder, he quickly levered a 7.62 mm round into the breech and set his right eye to the Starlite night scope, using the laser image enhancer to focus on the sec men across the valley.

They were about six hundred yards away.

Ryan waited.

He'd waved Doc on, to make sure the rig kept moving steadily ahead. As far as Ryan knew, there wasn't any way for the pursuing sec men to loop around and get ahead of them. But he wasn't about to take that chance.

Four hundred yards.

The night scope and the image enhancer brought the posse of Sidler's men much closer.

At three hundred yards Ryan could have guaranteed to put down at least a couple of the men or their horses. But there was no reason to open fire until they were real close.

One hundred and fifty yards.

Ryan waited, steadying his breathing, slowing his heartbeat.

The nearest horseman was now within a hundred paces of where he stood, riding at a steady pace, halfway between a walk and a canter.

"Fish in a barrel," Ryan whispered as his finger took up the slack on the trigger of the Steyr. The weapon fired, and the one-eyed man felt the jolt run up his arm to his shoulder.

The spent round ejected and tinkled onto the frozen pebbles by his boots.

His eye went back to the targets. He didn't bother to check what had happened to the first man he'd fired at, knowing with absolute certainty that he was already down and done with a high-velocity bullet through his head.

The second round picked off the sec man at the back of the group, his horse rearing and whinnying in terror at the noise and the hot smell of spilled blood.

As he'd intended, those two rounds threw the pursuit into total chaos.

He looked up from the scope, seeing that the

front horse had toppled off the path, crashing and screaming through the brush toward the narrow, fast-flowing river. The rider that Ryan had shot second had gone down, bringing his mount with him, blocking the trail to the rear.

"Never, never kill, just for the sake of the killing rush in your blood."

The Trader had hammered that into any new recruits who joined the war wags.

Ryan hesitated for a moment before shooting the sec man who was trying to get some order in the terrified chaos. The bullet hit him through the throat, smashing his spine and lifting him out of the saddle.

Then, without another glance, Ryan slung the Steyr across his shoulder, climbed onto the skewbald and rejoined the others a quarter mile farther south.

ELLIE HAD BEEN KEEPING a careful watch on the prisoners. Ryan had said that she no longer needed to knock them out the moment they recovered consciousness again.

"Just let them know that you'll hit them if they try and talk or make any kind of sound. That's all you need to do."

As they rode on through the night, they saw no more signs of pursuers.

J.B. came back from point to walk his bay mare alongside Ryan's mount. "Looks like we got away free."

"Don't count your fishes until they're in the cooking pot." Ryan watched as Doc heeled his towering stallion to the back of the rig. Ellie appeared, leaning on the tailboard, talking to the old man. Both of them were laughing.

"Keep an eye on those killers, Ellie," J.B. called.

But it was Baron Wizard Sidler who made the move, wriggling unnoticed, working the baling wire over his sweating and bloodied wrists.

If he'd been patient and freed some of the others, the story would have had a different ending.

But he couldn't wait for his vengeance.

Chapter Thirty-Nine

The elderly dowager stood trembling by her chair, holding out her bloodstained hands to the gigantic figure of the baron, who was frozen in the doorway, staring at the bizarre tableau.

"I'm sorry, son," she whispered.

"What the fuck is this?" His voice sounded like a puzzled little boy's. "Come on, Mother. What the fuck is all this? What's happened?"

The cavalry saber rattled against a chair as he turned sharply, his hand falling to the pearl butt of the Smith & Wesson Magnum.

"They've tried…" the dowager began, her fingers twitching, as if she were practicing to play a musical instrument.

Krysty was holding the little .22 pistol, with three of its rounds spent. She was standing close to the fire. Mildred was closer to the door, one arm on Dean's shoulder.

The boy held his slim-bladed dagger in front of him. There were a few drops of vermilion blood on the steel, tinted golden by the flames of the blazing logs.

"Mother!" The single word was roared out.

Her fingers dripped crimson, the spots pattering around her feet onto the fur rug. Blood was running over her hand, down her arm.

"I told them…Alferd."

"Told them what?"

Krysty answered. "Told us that you wanted Dean for your own son. Wanted to fuck us and get more sons."

Mildred's voice was cold. "And she said that you planned to cross John and Ryan and the others. Murder them, even if they brought you back the prisoners you wanted from Yuma. It's true, isn't it?"

The great head turned toward her, the white beard stained with a thread of spittle. The eyes were wide open, staring at the black woman.

"My mother told you all of this? I don't believe you."

"It's true, son. I was going to make them do like…like you wanted."

"I heard shots. Two or three."

Dean spoke up, his voice shrill with shock. "The old bitch tried to chill Krysty and Mildred. So I stabbed her."

"You stabbed my mother...." The baron laughed. "Never. But the blood?"

The dowager lifted her left hand, showing the clotted darkness that was seeping from a slit in her dress near the armpit. "Such a small knife, Alferd, with a pretty green hilt. Like those necklaces I used to collect from olden times."

Her voice was gradually fading away.

"It's true!" he said, incredulous.

"The bitch had it coming. I hope her ghost never finds itself any fucking rest." Dean spit on the palm of his hand and made the sign of the cross toward the dying woman.

Nelson actually staggered as though someone had struck him in the face. "You told them the truth, Mother! The bloody bastard truth!"

He drew the big blaster, cocked and fired it in a single fluid movement.

The bullet hit the dowager in the chest, slightly to the left of her breastbone, lifting her off her feet and throwing her in tottering, stumbling steps toward the fire.

Krysty dodged her, keeping both eyes on the baron, the little pistol feeling like a child's toy against the seven-and-a-half-foot giant.

The only thing that stopped her from opening fire was the knowledge that it would almost certainly seal the death warrants for all three of them.

Their chances of escaping alive from the ville, having murdered Baron Nelson, were just about as good as turning shit into gold.

"Life comes way down near the bottom of the totem pole," Nelson said in a strange, whispering kind of voice.

"That's true, Chief," Mildred replied, unable to look away from the hearth where the jerking corpse of the dowager had finally toppled face-down into the fire. Her long hair had blazed like a magnesium flare, making the air in the room stink.

"Can't we pull her away?" Dean asked.

The baron shook his head, smiling with a sightless, simpering idiocy. "No. The wicked burn in hell. Mother told me that, always. Wizard Sidler and his killers will burn when... Burn slowly. Listen," he said, nodding as though he could hear the beat of a different drum. "Listen to skin crack and eyeballs pop."

The intensity of the man's madness held them all in silence.

The stench of roasting flesh was nauseating. Though she was obviously dead, the horror was magnified by the old woman's feet and legs still moving, as if she were considering lifting her face from the ferocious heat.

"Now what, Baron?"

The eyes turned toward Krysty. "Such beautiful

hair, my dear lady. If we have a son, will his hair glow like living flames? It is so vivid and brilliant, it almost seems to be alive.''

Krysty could feel her sentient hair moving, packing itself protectively around the back of her neck, every strand sensitive to the danger in the room.

''You have three little pellets of lead in that tiny blaster, Krysty.'' Now the huge madman was sounding like a wise and benevolent uncle, with a stubborn and slightly foolish niece. ''It won't harm me, but it might make me very cross. Might make me want to take off your clothes, remove your tight, silken panties, that fit so snugly between the cleft of your firm buttocks... And then—''

''Shut your filthy mouth!'' Dean had taken three angry steps across the room, threatening the baron with his knife.

''A toy pistol and a babe's bodkin! I tremble with terror, boy.''

''My knife was enough to chill your bitch-mother, and it can do the same for you, you shit-mouthed triple-sick bastard.''

The barrel of the Magnum slithered around until it snarled at the boy.

''Now that wasn't the way a child should speak to his father,'' Nelson chided.

''I'd never speak to my father like that.''

For a moment the big man looked puzzled. "Not your father is... What?" The hand holding the gun began to shake.

Krysty licked her lips, steadying the .22 on the baron's face.

Nelson wrinkled his nose. "Stink of charred flesh! Typical of the old shitbag! Hated her. Now she's told you everything. Suppose I'd best chill you all now. Except the boy. Yeah, now."

Chapter Forty

It was one hour and seventeen minutes into the tenth and final day of the mission.

They'd been making good time, along a trail that was scarcely dusted with snow. The mud and slush had frozen, turning into ruts that jarred and jolted the wag.

Michael had heeled his burro out to the point position; Capestrano and Knuckles were on the rig's narrow seat; Ellie and Doc were chatting over the tailboard, and Ryan and J.B. were walking their horses about thirty paces behind.

Too far behind to be able to do anything to prevent the tragedy from unfolding in front of their eyes.

It was only afterward that it was possible to trace the steps—Sidler wriggling free of the baling wire around his wrists, ignoring an urgent, whispered entreaty from Jim Jennison to play it cool and careful, and free them all.

He saw the backs of Capestrano and Knuckles, the latter with the taped hilt of a short-bladed skinning knife showing at his belt. Ellie was involved in a coquettish conversation with Doc, assuming that everything was still safely under her control.

Wizard Sidler snatched out the knife, hesitating for a fraction of a second. His lips were pulled back in a feral snarl as he stared at the two men on the driving seat. But there was only one person guarding the rear of the rig, and that was the treacherous actress.

The baron lunged toward Ellie, slipping as he trod on Julio, nearly falling over Twenty Gooseneck's outstretched legs.

Ryan heard the beginning of Knuckles's belated shout of warning as he felt his knife being stripped from its sheath.

Ellie started around, the smile still pinned to her face. Doc stood in the stirrups, then his hand fell toward the polished butt of the Let Mat, the old man moving faster than Ryan had ever seen him move before.

Then there was the shadow from beneath the canvas hood, its teeth glittering in the moonlight, the steel blinking coldly.

Knuckles's shout reached everyone. "He's got my knife!"

Doc's blaster cleared leather as both Ryan and J.B. went for their weapons.

They weren't fast enough.

Wizard Sidler opened Ellie's throat from ear to ear, slashing backhanded, the blade severing flesh and arteries and cutting open the woman's windpipe.

Ellie's hands reached out to Doc, her blond hair streaming around her as she struggled for air, air that came swamped in thick gobbets of blood.

Sidler grinned triumphantly, pushing the dying woman over the tailgate of the wag, where she fell into the furrowed, icy mud. Ellie fought her way to her hands and knees, but the arterial blood was pumping out of her, and what remained of her life was measured in slackening beats of the heart.

Ryan had the SIG-Sauer out, ready to put a 9 mm full-metal jacket through Sidler's right shoulder, taking him safely out of action without jeopardizing their mission.

But he hadn't reckoned on Doc's unprecedented combat speed. It was as if the world had slowed down and time was dragging its feet.

Knuckles was hauling desperately on the reins, the horses rearing in protest. Monsignor Diego Capestrano was screaming at the top of his voice, in a bizarre, fluting falsetto, reacting to what he'd glimpsed going down just behind him.

Michael was slowest to react, half turning in the saddle of the swaybacked mule.

Jennison's voice rose from the bed of the wag. "Stick 'em all, Wizard!"

J.B.'s Uzi was in his hand, but Doc was directly in his line of fire.

Ryan saw the Le Mat leveling toward the yelping face of the exultant baron, the .63-caliber scattergun round beneath the hammer.

The range was less than ten feet.

"No, Doc! Don't kill him or—"

The rest of the sentence vanished in the roar of the blaster, Sidler disappearing in the mushrooming cloud of black powder smoke.

Of all the people that Ryan had ridden with in his life, Dr. Theophilus Tanner had to be about the worst shot. But with a Le Mat, at ten feet, it truly didn't matter.

The shell exploded and the shards of lead starred out, striking Baron Wizard Sidler in the center of his face.

It was like hitting a big, ripe watermelon with a sixteen-pound sledgehammer.

The head evaporated into splinters of bone, gruel of blood and pulped eyes and lacerated skin. Several of the man's shattered teeth tore tiny holes through the canvas top of the wag. Capestrano screamed even more loudly as a jagged fragment of jawbone clipped him on the upper arm, ripping his shirt and drawing blood.

The headless corpse remained upright for a supernatural moment or two before the rocking of the rig sent it folding on top of the five bound prisoners.

"Shit," Ryan said, holstering the SIG-Sauer. "Fireblast and *shit!*"

There was shouting and confusion inside the wag, as the five prisoners found themselves with a blood-sodden body kicking and rolling all over them.

It took several minutes for Knuckles to control the terrified horses, and for Capestrano to realize that he wasn't badly hurt, but that Ellie was dead.

J.B. and Michael heaved out the decapitated trunk of Sidler and dumped it by the side of the track, leaving it for the scavengers of the forest to find and remove.

Ellie's body was tidied and laid on the ground while they decided what to do with it.

Doc had dismounted and wandered off into the trees, where Ryan followed him. He discovered the old man sitting against the trunk of a massive live oak, his knees drawn up under the chin, his right hand still gripping the Le Mat.

He heard Ryan's boots crunching toward him through the frozen mud and looked up, tears glistening on his lined cheeks.

"My dear fellow," he began.

"No, Doc." Ryan hunkered down beside him. "Definitely not. I don't want to hear it."

"I've sentenced Krysty, Mildred and the boy to death. Perhaps to a fate that might prove worse than dying."

"No choice."

"I should have shot sooner."

"None of us guessed that Sidler could get free. My fault, more than yours."

Doc shook his head. "I appreciate your kind efforts to remove some part of the stigma from my shoulders to yours, Ryan, but I fear that I really cannot allow it."

"Look, the bastard chilled Ellie, right in front of all of us. I'd have gunned him down, if you hadn't gotten in first, Doc."

"Truly?"

Ryan patted him on the arm. "Sure. Good shot, too, from the back of a horse at a moving target. Real good shooting."

"But what about our friends in Vista ville, Ryan? Our friends. Our companions. Our colleagues. Our fellow travelers. Our…" He stopped, wiping away a fresh trickle of tears. "Oh, by the Three Kennedys! But I am *so* sorry."

"Look, we had a deal with Baron Nelson. Bring back Sidler with two of his son's butchers. Or bring back four of the others. Alive. Well, we got five of them. Long as we get back to the ville by dawn tomorrow we'll be fine. Got us around thirty more hours. We can just do it.''

Doc stood shakily, accepting Ryan's hand. ''You know that the lady and I... Being a gentleman, I would never have mentioned it, of course. But in the light of what has transpired, I feel that it is no longer a betrayal of confidence. She and I were, briefly but memorably, lovers.''

Ryan managed to fake surprise. ''No! That so, Doc? You sly old son of a bitch!''

''Not so old, Ryan. Yes, we were and... You see, Ryan—'' Doc dropped his voice to a whisper ''—you remember that I was once very close to little Lori Quint. You recall the child?''

''Some child, Doc. She was taller than you.''

''And she died.''

''We all do, Doc.''

''I know. But she died quite horribly, before my eyes.''

''Yeah. I see what you're saying. So did Ellie.''

''Correct. Perhaps I am some sort of a jinx. A Jonah. A taboo creature. A dark angel. A bringer of death. A destroyer of worlds.''

''No, Doc. Just that we both live in Deathlands. If I started thinking about all the good friends I've lost, I'd never sleep. Go hang myself from the nearest tree. Or swallow my blaster.''

"I suppose that is so. But it was so appalling to see her throat open like... Someone once told me that if you choose to always look back, then you become as dead as a beaver hat."

"So, let's go on."

"Bury her first, Ryan?"

"Time's tight, Doc."

"Please."

Chapter Forty-One

The bedrock was close to the surface, and it was hard work to scrape out a shallow depression to lay the small corpse in.

Diego had wrapped Ellie in a cloak of scarlet silk, gently covering her face. "Can't bear the idea of the dirt landing in her eyes," he said.

Doc insisted on carrying the body to the makeshift, hasty grave. "She's so light," he said hoarsely. "Barely a handful of feathers."

"She was dying of rad cancer," Knuckles muttered. "We all knew it. Another two or three months was all they reckoned she got. Me's glad, sort of, she went quick and not much pain."

They took turns to shovel in some of the cold earth, until the bright red material had vanished, then piled on heavy stones from a rough outcrop at the foot of the cliff to their left.

"Better get going," Ryan warned. "Time's passing. You checked the rest of them, J.B.? Make sure nobody else gets free."

"All secure," the Armorer said. "Trouble is,

that baling wire won't hold forever. They keep working at it, and it'll weaken. Need keeping a good eye on until we reach the ville."

Capestrano half lifted a hand. "I wish to say a few words, Ryan."

"Quickly."

"It will take no more than a couple of minutes, I promise."

"Go on."

The horses were all tethered to the rear of the wag as the small group of men stood around the grave, all hatless, their breaths mingling, white in the moonlight.

As he spoke, his voice rich and sonorous, the stout little man seemed to grow in stature, the ancient words from the Shakespeare play, *The Tempest*, filling the clearing.

"Our revels now are ended. These our actors,
As I foretold you, were all spirits and
Are melted into air, into thin air:
And, like the baseless fabric of this vision,
The cloud-capp'd towers, the gorgeous palaces,
The solemn temples, the great globe itself,
Yea, all which it inherit, shall dissolve
And, like this insubstantial pageant faded,
Leave not a rack behind."

Capestrano paused, blowing his nose on his sleeve and wiping his eyes with the back of his hand. "Sorry, Ellie," he whispered. "Not very professional. Crying like this."

Ryan tried to angle the face of his wrist chron to catch the time. They needed to be moving on as soon as possible.

But Diego was nearly done.

As he came to the ending of Prospero's great, final speech, the deep, rounded voice of Doc Tanner joined him.

"We are such stuff
As dreams are made of, and our little life
Is ended with a sleep."

In the stillness, there was only Knuckles's soft voice. "Good night, Ellie."

WITHIN A FEW MINUTES of their leaving the burial site, the skies clouded from the east. The moon vanished, and the trail immediately became almost invisible.

And it began to snow again, large wet flakes that clung to the face and drifted into open mouths, filling in the ruts in the track, making it impossible for Knuckles to try to steer a smooth course. The wag jolted and jarred, sending the five prisoners rolling and protesting from side to side and front to back.

As a precaution, J.B. had let Michael ride his own horse, the burro trailing mournfully behind the rig, while he perched near the rear, eyes never leaving the quintet of killers.

Jim Jennison was nearest. He had a deep purple bruise across his face that had almost closed his left eye. He lay awkwardly, knees up, half on his side, his tied hands behind him.

"You could help me sit up, brother," he said to J.B.

"Not your brother, Jennison."

"Near as makes no odds."

"Not true."

"You don't talk much, do you, John?" He laughed. "Like your father. Seems he wasn't much into speaking, either."

"You got something you really want to say to me, Jennison, then you best get to it. Time's near done for you."

"Nelson'll torture us, John."

"Sure."

"You don't give a flying fuck, do you?"

"No."

"Riding all those years with the Trader and that ice-heart Cawdor! Changed you. For the worst, brother."

"You and the others slaughtered a little boy, Jennison."

"Father's a triple bastard."

"Doesn't matter. Not when you go out, six of you grown, and butcher a child. Don't visit the sins of the father on the children. Talk's never goin' to make it right."

"Well, fuck you, brother. You're going to be chilled real soon."

Doc had ridden in close and heard the end of the conversation. He laughed at Jennison. "I vow it's truth you say. I may die tomorrow, but you will die today." He paused. "I doubt that I got that quote just right. But it's near enough for scum like you, Jennison."

THE SNOW GREW WORSE, and their progress grew slower.

Ryan walked his skewbald ahead, trying to break trail and make it easier for the wag. When he finally managed to make out the time from his wrist chron, he was shocked to find how late it had become.

When the others caught up with him, he shouted to Knuckles, still at the reins, "Gotta go faster. Still miles to go and we're running out of time."

"Me can't hardly see the road!"

"Follow me. I'll keep in sight so's you can see which way the track goes."

There was very little wind, but the snow was falling more heavily, huge lumps of whiteness that seemed to hang in the cold air between the tall pines. Ryan kept glancing back over his shoulder, constantly having to ease the patch over his left eye as water seeped behind it.

He could hear the hooves clattering on the packed earth and the jingling of the harness, Knuckles calling out softly to encourage the tiring animals.

"Come on, beauties. Few more steps and then it's sweet hay and good water. Warm stall and soft bedding. Come on, my beauties."

Capestrano was hunched alongside the young man on the seat, his face turned inward. He'd hardly spoken since Ellie's brutal murder.

Doc heeled his stallion forward, to pick its way delicately through the blanket of snow.

"We shall make it with a good margin to spare, my dear Ryan," he said. "I have every confidence in your ability to bring home the bacon. You have never failed yet."

"Long as Nelson keeps his word."

"You fear treachery? By the Three Kennedys, I had not thought of that."

"You look at any baron and you see a man

whose mind is locked into perpetual darkness, a man who would cheerfully slit the throat of his own mother if it helped him gain or hold power, Doc.''

''There has been too much slitting of throats, Ryan. Far too much.'' He paused. They were entering a particularly narrow section of the trail. ''You know that Mistress Ellie Morte... Her name, Morte. It means death.''

But Ryan Cawdor didn't have any time to ponder on that extraordinary fact.

Behind him, the lords of chaos had decided to enter the game.

IN THE BED OF THE WAG, Jim Jennison had suddenly begun to scream virulent abuse at his half brother.

''You piss-drinking little sheepfucker! You gotta save me. Let the rest die, John, but fucking save me!''

J.B. ignored him, but Knuckles was startled and turned around in the seat, fearing an escape attempt was beginning.

As he moved, he accidentally tugged on the reins, bringing the heads of the horses around to the right, toward the edge of a drop camouflaged by a bank of fresh snow.

The front wheel of the rig slithered away from

the cliff on their left toward the sheer drop on the other side, slipping through the crust of snow like a knife through parchment.

Knuckles had a fraction of a second to save them from disaster.

He stood, sawing at the reins, trying to heave the horses around to the left, away from the sighing abyss. But his boots slipped in the icy slush and he half fell, knocking into Diego Capestrano, who screamed and clutched at his arm, knocking him totally off balance.

Michael yelled a belated warning as he saw the canvas-topped wag begin to slide inexorably toward the right, the rear wheel teetering on the brink for a heart-stopping moment.

Then it went over.

J.B. did a back flip off the tail, landing in a crouch, the Uzi ready for action.

Reena Miller managed to get to her feet, standing spread-legged in the bed of the wag, her mouth open in a silent rictus of terror.

Capestrano dived clumsily off the side, landing with a jolt on the edge of the trail.

Ryan turned his horse, watching helplessly as the rig slipped ponderously away, the horses' hooves scrabbling helplessly for a purchase. It began to roll down the steep hillside, Knuckles still hanging on to the reins.

Chapter Forty-Two

Nelson filled the room, his seven and a half feet towering above the two women and the boy. Three hundred pounds of mostly solid muscle and bone moved ponderously toward Krysty, who was nearest to him.

"Pull your flame-bright head off your shoulders and piss down your neck," he said. "Then rip the face off the black bitch." He smiled broadly, his mouth visible among the acres of white beard. "After that, the boy's all mine."

"What about my father?"

Nelson stopped a moment, looking puzzled. "You know the answer to that, little man. He's dead. Probably dead up in Yuma a week ago. But even if he made it through there, the moment he sets foot in Vista he's cold meat."

"Says you, shit for brains." The boy threw the baron the finger.

The room was filling with coils of foul-smelling smoke from the smoldering corpse in the grate.

Krysty kept the little pistol leveled in her hand,

knowing that the question of Ryan's arrival back at the ville had become academic. Whatever happened was going down right now, between the four of them.

Alferd Nelson half drew the Magnum, the mother-of-pearl handle glinting in the golden glow of the oil lamps. Krysty's finger tightened on the narrow spur trigger of the .22.

But the man laughed, a great booming yelp of merriment. "No! Not the bullet. Not for two shrinking gaudy sluts. No, that would be a waste of jack on them. *This* is for whores." He drew the saber in a whisper of death. "Clean cold steel is best for filthy, hot slag bitches."

"Take him now, Krysty," Mildred said. "No choices left."

A DOZEN MILES to the north Ryan swung from the saddle of the skewbald, looping the reins over a young piñon and drawing the SIG-Sauer from its holster.

"Fireblast!" he cursed, watching Capestrano's wag plunge from sight over the edge of the wooded valley.

There was a sharp crack of splintered bone, and one of the two draft horses stopped screaming in terror. A tangled cacophony of yelling and cursing overrode the sound of the rig breaking apart as it rolled down the steep slope toward the narrow river at its bottom.

Michael had toppled off his borrowed mount, while Doc was fighting to manage his own stallion. The black horse was rearing, white-eyed, and it was all the old man could do to control it and save himself a bad fall.

The noise from the ravine had stopped.

The wag had become jammed on its side, about sixty feet down, between two large ponderosas. One horse was clearly dead, its head thrown back on its neck at a hideously unnatural angle. The other animal was barely moving, feebly kicking its hind legs, which were tangled in the traces. The main shaft of the wag had broken, and two of the wheels had sheared off, one of them still rolling drunkenly toward the water.

The canvas top was torn, but it was so dark, with the snow billowing all around, that Ryan couldn't make out what was happening below him.

He could make out the shape of what he guessed was Knuckles, lying sprawled close to the wreckage. As he stared into the gloom, the figure moved and staggered clumsily to its feet. One arm seemed to be hanging limply at his side.

"You all right?" Ryan shouted.

"Me arm's broken, and me think that a leg's busted and all." The voice was strong and clear.

"Goes with me hunched back and me scarred face." His laugh sounded strained. "Me never did have much luck, Ryan."

"Get up here, if you can," J.B. called. "Make it fast. Bastards in the rig could be getting themselves free."

"If they survived," Michael added, joining them on the furrowed edge of the trail. "Terrible accident."

"At least they will have no armaments, will they?" Doc had won his battle with his horse and also stood alongside the others, the Le Mat clutched in his hand.

"There any blasters in the rig, Knuckles?" Ryan yelled.

"Me can't get up." The lad obviously hadn't heard the question.

"I'll go help him," Michael offered.

"Wait a moment."

Raising his voice, Ryan said, "Knuckles, do you know if there are any blasters in the wag?"

"Yeah. Think there's a couple of pump-action shotguns inside. Want me to get them?"

"Yeah. No. No, Knuckles. Leave them be. Just try and get up to us."

J.B. glanced at him, snow smearing his glasses. "Those five bastards get their hands on those, we got us a firefight."

Ryan nodded. "Trouble is, friend, we're fucked, anyway."

"Why? Time?"

"Yeah. Never get them to Vista by dawn, on foot through this."

Far below them, Knuckles called out again. "Any chance of me getting a hand up?"

Michael looked at Ryan. "Let me and Doc go down."

"You and John Barrymore could keep us covered from up here if there's any danger from that evil quintet," Doc added. "We can't just leave that poor boy."

It was a razor-edge decision.

People like Jennison, Gooseneck and the others wouldn't just be lying down there waiting. They'd be working on getting free. Assuming that the rolling wag hadn't knocked them all unconscious.

The inside of the rig would be a shambles, with everything tossed everywhere. But professional killers would be able to scent a firearm at a hundred paces through a dust storm.

"No, don't go down."

"I protest most strongly, my dear fellow," Doc said.

"We all go down together, slow and careful. And keep an eye on the wag."

Knuckles stood and waited patiently, leaning

against a lightning-scarred redwood, his upturned face a pale blur in the night.

"Spread out in a skirmish line," Ryan ordered. "J.B., take the left. Watch your footing and keep watching the wag."

The trapped horse had begun to kick more vigorously, its whinnying rising up the scale toward a full-fledged scream.

The ground was treacherous, plowed up by the tumbling wag, muddy and icy. It took a deal of concentration to avoid a fall.

There had been no sound of movement from inside the rig, the stained canvas stretched tight over the iron frame.

Suddenly, silently, a silver knife point appeared and quickly slashed the coarse material from top to bottom.

"Watch it!" Ryan shouted.

Knuckles began to turn to look behind him at the wag.

THE FIRST .22-caliber bullet hit Baron Alferd Nelson through the shoulder, lower and to the right of where Krysty had aimed.

But it still made him take a faltering, uncertain step to his right, nearly dropping the saber. He grunted with pain or surprise.

"Mistake, doing that. Now it'll be a slow killing

for you, bitch!'' But it was said with a jolly, twin-kling smile.

"Again," Mildred urged.

"Blaster's not accurate."

"And that was the last bullet, my dear. Dear Mama only ever bothered to load in four of the little pea-poppers."

"Lying bastard," Dean spit. "Let him have it, Krysty."

Nelson stood and bowed, presenting the sword with a flourish, as though he were playing a court-ier in some antique vid. "Yes. Let me have it, Krysty. Then I'll let you have it. Your delightful, fire-braided head can decorate the main gate into the ville."

As he took another step toward her, Krysty pulled the trigger again, trying to compensate for the pocket blaster's lack of accuracy.

The hammer clicked on an empty chamber, and the baron slapped his thigh with delight.

"Didn't I tell you, bitch? Only four rounds and they're all gone. You made your useless play and you lost!"

Blood trickled steadily from the tiny black hole in his shoulder, but it didn't bother him at all. No more than a hammer's blow on the armored flank of a war wag.

Krysty thumbed back the hammer for a sixth

time—for the last time—took aim at the center of the arrogant, sneering face and pulled the trigger.

JENNISON WAS FIRST OUT through the torn canvas, squeezing off a round from the scattergun he held at the hip. He hit the steep slope running, feet slipping as he scurried for cover.

Julio was second out, holding a knife, followed by Ossie Grant. He struggled for balance as he landed in the snow-covered mud, giving Ryan time to shoot him through the stomach and again through the side of the head as he collapsed to the ground.

Jennison fired a second time at the four men moving down the steep side of the valley. They dived for cover, giving Gooseneck and Reena time to scuttle from the back of the rig, the woman limping heavily as she ran for safety.

Ryan had flattened himself behind a live oak, squinting to one side of the gnarled trunk, and, seeing, to his horror, that Knuckles remained standing in the open.

"Get down!" he yelled, waving with the muzzle of the SIG-Sauer.

The woman saw him and tried a shot, the starring lead ripping through the snow-covered branches just above Ryan's head.

Doc and J.B. were holding fire, unable to get a

clear shot through the driving snow and the clustering trees.

"Knuckles, get down!"

Ryan's shout had no effect. The hunchbacked lad had turned away and was hopping toward the wag, where Reena and Gooseneck had taken cover.

When Knuckes was only a couple of stumbling steps away, the woman appeared, hair matted and tangled with the snow, and leveled the scattergun.

Chapter Forty-Three

The .22 revolver misfired, the hammer falling with a halfhearted click.

Nelson roared with maniac laughter. "Off with your head, bitch!"

Krysty fumbled, trying to thumb the hammer back for a last, desperate attempt. There was a round in the chamber; she could see that.

The baron hefted the saber above his head, taking a shuffling step that brought him within reach of the woman.

Dean was fastest.

He hurled himself at Nelson, like a human projectile, the knife held out in front of him as he dived. It struck the giant just above the left knee, the point grating off bone. Dean let go and rolled to one side, dodging the furious kick, seeing the turquoise hilt of his knife glowing in the baron's thigh.

"Fucking little..." He lowered the long blade and stooped to pluck out the dagger.

Krysty saw her chance.

Instead of retreating, the woman advanced, ramming the muzzle of the tiny revolver into the bending baron's open mouth.

The tip of the foresight broke a splinter off one of the man's front teeth.

Nelson still laughed, clamping his powerful jaws on the steel barrel. For a crazed moment Krysty had a vision of him biting through it.

He swung back his right arm, still holding the brass hilt of the saber, tattered velvet ribbons of gold and maroon thread dangling from the guard.

Krysty pulled the trigger.

KNUCKLES WAS LIFTED OFF his feet by the force of the blast. The shot struck him at point-blank range, the concentrated pellets of lead driving into the center of his chest with devastating power.

For Ryan and the others, watching from fifty feet higher up the hill, it was as though a giant hand had pushed its way straight through Knuckles's body. A great spray of blood and flesh erupted from between the lad's deformed shoulders, bursting black upon the fallen snow.

He spun with a bizarre, balletic elegance, more graceful in his dying than he had ever been in his life.

"Got the crip!" Reena whooped triumphantly, holding the scattergun over her head.

"Bitch," J.B. breathed.

The Uzi was on full-auto, and he squeezed the trigger, twenty rounds of 9 mm ammo tearing the woman apart.

The power of the full-metal jackets hurled her against the side of the covered wag, her blood fountaining across the torn canvas. Reena's arms were spread wide, like an obscene parody of a crucified Christ.

"Let's go get the other three," Ryan said. "Right now."

THE CRACK OF THE PISTOL was absurdly quiet. Baron Alferd Nelson's mouth muffled the explosion of the last bullet so that it sounded no louder than a rat farting in an empty barn.

Krysty let go of the patterned butt, feeling blood and saliva trickling across her hand. The revolver dropped to the floor, bouncing and then lying still by her boots.

"What the fuck have you done?" Nelson asked, his deep-set eyes bewildered as he lifted his left hand to his bleeding lips. "What?"

Krysty had already moved out of range of the long sword. Dean and Mildred stood together, close to the door into the room.

"You should've kept your word."

She looked at the others, speaking quickly and

quietly. "Don't know how much the bullet's done. Get ready to run for it. Don't wait."

Nelson sat suddenly on the floor, like a dozen sacks of coal being dumped at once. The saber clattered away from him, but he ignored the weapon. He was exploring the inside of his mouth, like someone with a severe toothache.

His words were barely audible. "You done something bad. Something in...inside my brain. Feel something leaking in my fucking head."

Mildred stepped closer, kneeling to stare closely at the wounded colossus. "Hemorrhage from someplace behind the roof of his mouth. He's bleeding from the ears and eyes as well."

"What's that mean?" Dean asked. "Could get his blaster and chill him, real easy. Want me to do that, Krysty?"

"No. But you can drag the old woman's body out of the fire. Flowers in the vase on that table. Pour the water on her. Put out the flames, Dean."

The boy went immediately, helped by Mildred, and tugged the dowager's corpse away by the ankles. The cold water hissed and spit on her charred flesh, but the smoke diminished and the stench became a little less vile.

Alferd Nelson took no notice of them. He'd slithered down until he was lying flat on his back, both hands clasping his cheeks. More and more blood seeped between his fingers, and his eyes had become dark pits of crimson.

The baron tried to speak, but he was no longer making any kind of sense.

"Tomorrow's another now. Your answer do. He's gone, gone always gone."

Mildred touched Krysty on the arm. "Nearly done," she whispered. "Why am I whispering? He can't hear me and there's just us here."

"Only a matter of time before the sec men come calling." Krysty looked around the room. "Ryan'll be here by dawn. Best find a place to hole up until then, I guess."

JIM JENNISON, Julio and Twenty Gooseneck had three knives and a single pump-action scattergun between them.

Ryan made Michael go back onto the road, out of danger.

"Want to get them."

"Then, you need a blaster. Not now. Doc?"

"Yes?"

"Stay here, near the top. Watch for any of them trying to break around us and get to the horses. Don't hesitate to chill them."

"Worry not on that score, old friend."

It was easy.

The three survivors were hardened killers, but

they had no chance against Ryan and J.B. Their experience of ambushes and firefights, combined with their overwhelming superiority in weapons, meant that Jennison and the others were dead meat.

Ryan edged around to the right while J.B. took the left. They kept cover between themselves and where they'd last spotted Jennison with the 12-gauge.

"Ryan," the Armorer whispered.

"What?"

"Sure you want them chilled?"

"Damned right. Too late to try and barter them with Nelson. Just take them out and leave the place a little cleaner."

Julio made his break first, running and tumbling down the slope, hoping to make it into the brush beside the water.

At thirty yards Ryan was able to put a 7.62 mm round through the back of the man's skull, blasting away most of his face. Julio went down like a brain-dead rabbit, flailing and kicking in the undergrowth.

Jennison retaliated by pumping out three blind rounds from the shotgun, but Ryan and J.B. were well hidden.

The mutie, Twenty Gooseneck, nearly took them by surprise.

Instead of trying to escape, he came straight at

them, arms waving, clutching a butcher's cleaver, mouth wide open in a scream of hatred.

Ryan was still holding the Steyr, and the sudden charge by the web-fingered mutie caught him cold. He snapped off a shot, but it missed by several inches. J.B. opened up with the Uzi, but the trees that sheltered them from Jennison also protected Gooseneck from his fire.

The 9 mm bullets plowed up a furrow of mud and ice, all around the killer's feet, but he was untouched.

"Bastards!"

He was too fast for Ryan to be able to level the Steyr for a second shot. So he waited for a heartbeat or two, holding the rifle at the high port. As Gooseneck closed with him, swinging back the cleaver to split him from throat to groin, Ryan whipped the butt of the blaster around in a short, vicious arc.

The walnut stock impacted with Gooseneck's chin, splitting the bone and separating upper and lower jaws. Teeth cracked and tumbled out on a tsunami of bright blood.

The mutie staggered backward, barely keeping his balance, the cleaver falling into the trampled and bloodied snow.

J.B. killed him with two rounds through the chest.

The clearing was still, silent apart from the muted whinnying of the surviving draft horse.

The Armorer unslung the Smith & Wesson M-4000 model, glancing across at Ryan. "This part of it's mine, understand?"

"Sure. I'm here to cover you."

J.B. nodded. "Hell, I know that." He raised his voice. "Come on out, Jennison. It's all over. All done."

"Fuck you, brother. You come down here and take me."

"Intend to. And, I'm not your brother, Jennison. For the last time."

Ryan watched, the Steyr at his shoulder, conscious of Michael and Doc behind him at the top of the slope.

J.B. climbed down with a wonderful delicacy and economy of movement, carefully placing one boot in front of the other, keeping his balance, steadying himself before taking another step.

Always keeping the trees between him and his waiting half brother.

Jennison's nerve cracked.

"Here!" He threw out the pump-action shotgun so that it landed near the wag. "I'm coming, John. Don't shoot."

"Blaster empty, is it?" J.B. called, stopping for

a moment to wipe more snow from his wire-rimmed spectacles.

"Fuck you. Here I am, brother."

Ryan steadied the laser-enhanced scope on the pale, short figure. Jennison had his hands raised, squinting eyes fixed on J. B. Dix. For a fleeting moment Ryan had the illusion that it was J.B. who filled the scope sight on the rifle.

"Drop the knife, right now, Jennison," J.B. ordered, the barrel of his scattergun gaping like a railroad tunnel.

"Knife, brother?"

Ryan had known John Barrymore Dix for a dozen years, knew him better than he'd ever known anyone in his life.

He had a flash of what was going to happen, certain about it in his heart.

"What knife, brother?" Jennison's voice grated at the nerves.

J.B.'s voice was infinitely weary. "It doesn't matter, brother."

He had the pistol grip in the scattergun firmly in his hand, the folding butt braced tight against his hip.

"It doesn't matter," he repeated.

And pulled the trigger.

The M-4000 held eight rounds of the Remington fléchettes, each round packed with twenty of the inch-long darts.

"Jesus," Michael breathed.

Chapter Forty-Four

Rick Coburn's slitted eyes showed no emotion at all. He stood on the balcony outside the main dining room of Vista ville, the first faltering light of the false dawn striking at the left side of his face.

"The time's nearly up for Ryan Cawdor to complete his part of the deal," he said. "Sunup on the tenth day."

Krysty shook her head. "How can you say that, knowing what you know?"

"How's that, lady? I know the baron's dead. Know you admit to chilling him with his mother's little toy blaster. And she's dead, too. Face burned away. You say that none of this is really your fault? Not *really* your fault, lady?"

"It's not," Dean insisted, stamping his foot. "You're triple stupe, if you don't see that, sec man."

"Now, how the sweet fuck do you figure that out, boy?"

Mildred answered him. "You were straight with us over the past ten days. But you were wrong,

Coburn. Wrong about your baron. He wasn't going
to keep his word. Why do you think he died?''

"Because someone put a .22-caliber bullet
through the roof of his mouth into his brain. Baron
must've been kneeling for anyone to do that.''

"Bending forward," Krysty said.

"Same difference." He looked away toward the
north. "Tell you the truth, I figured that Cawdor
might pull it off. Might bring Sidler back. Mebbe
some of his gang of killers.''

There was a silence while everyone considered
the implications.

Dawn.

Dawn on the last day, and no Ryan.

Krysty moved to stand directly in front of the
tall sec man, matching him for height. "You're
going to try for baron, aren't you?''

His eyes widened and his jaw dropped a little.
"You a seer, Krysty? Or a doomie? I haven't
breathed a word to anyone.''

"I just felt it, Coburn. Why not? Like you got
more honesty than nine-tenths of the barons I ever
heard about.''

"But that doesn't solve you. You two women
and the boy.''

"Let us go," Dean said.

"Can't.''

"Why?''

"You killed Nelson. Whole ville'll know that. They'll make an allowance for the way he acted. I can see to that. But it still means paying a blood price. Sec man's supposed to do something when his baron gets chilled. I have to do something."

"What? And when?" Mildred looked out across the snowy land, already tinted pink by the spreading light of the sun.

"Don't know. Hey, look at that. Heaven of a morning." He came close to smiling. "Stuff that dreams are made of."

"'WE ARE SUCH STUFF as dreams are made of, and our little life is ended with a sleep.'" Doc cleared his throat. "I thought that Diego and the poor lad, Knuckles, might appreciate it being said over them. As it was over Ellie."

Capestrano had broken his neck falling out of the wag, an instant and merciful passing.

Now he and Knuckles lay together on the bed of the wag, ready for Ryan to strike the match that would set the wreckage ablaze, and save the time and labor of a burying.

The killers lay where they had fallen, their stiffening corpses partly blanketed by the earlier snow.

"How late will we be, Ryan?" Michael asked. He couldn't keep his hands off his new possession. Tucked into the knotted rope belt was Julio's

Texas Longhorn Border Special, the small revolver that fired six rounds of centerfire .38s. The teenager had taken it from the saddle bags on J.B.'s bay mare, refusing what the Armorer insisted was a more useful blaster for him, Jim Jennison's own 9 mm Heckler & Koch 9-PS model.

"Hour or two late," Ryan replied.

"Not much."

"Enough, Michael, when you're dealing with a man like Alferd Nelson."

"So, what do we do?"

"Light this fire and move on. See what we see, and do what we do."

"I love it when you're runic, Ryan," Doc said, coming close to a smile.

"Hold the animals, Michael. In case the pyrotab startles them."

The tiny ignition device sparked first time, and Ryan dropped it into the pile of old theatrical costumes piled in a corner of the wag. The pale flame flickered and then caught.

Caesar's toga blazed and Lady Macbeth's nightgown disintegrated into flakes of charred blackness. A bag of assorted wigs and beards erupted like an emergency flare.

Within minutes the whole rig was burning fiercely from end to end.

"Let's go," Ryan said.

J.B. glanced around the hillside. "Just one more minute."

He walked away from the fierce heat of the flames, picking his way between the tangled, cold corpses of the five Yuma killers until he stood above the body of Jim Jennison, its gaping chest cavity blackened and crusted.

"You bastard," J.B. said very quietly and spit into the blank, milky eyes.

Behind him, the column of dark oily smoke from the wag was soaring into the fresh dawning.

DEAN POINTED OVER the heavy logs of the balcony. "Look."

Everyone turned, seeing a column of dark oily smoke soaring into the dawn sky.

"About ten miles north," Coburn said slowly. "Could be nothing."

"Could be Ryan and the others." Krysty shook her head. "If it is, then they'll be here in a couple of hours."

The sec boss didn't reply, staring out at the huge black finger that tainted the morning.

"Now what?" Mildred asked Coburn.

"If it's Ryan?"

"Course."

"Then I have to do some thinking. And him and me are going to have to do some talking."

He turned away and walked back into the room,
disappearing from view. Krysty caught Mildred's
eye and shrugged.

Chapter Forty-Five

The two men shook hands.

"That's the best deal I can do," Rick Coburn said. "I've spoken to some people and everyone agrees." He smiled thinly. "Well, most everyone agrees. One or two are for a swift hanging, but they got persuaded to think again."

"Two hours from the moment we clear the front gates of the ville?"

"Right. Then I lead the posse out after you. And there won't be any favors, Ryan. You all get weapons and a real good meal. And then supplies for three trail days."

Ryan nodded. "Fair enough. Better than fair. Appreciate it."

Coburn sniffed. "Never figured the old baron would have gone wolf-shit crazed."

"Happens. Sorry I didn't get any of the killers back here."

"Shit. They're dead and that's what matters. Sidler's death means life'll be a touch easier here in Vista. You done well, Ryan."

"Sure. Six coldhearts chilled. And three good folks down and done for. Could've been better."

The tall sec boss nodded. "Always could. But it could've been plenty worse."

THE PROMISED MEAL was excellent.

Ryan urged everyone to eat well, which was always common sense in Deathlands when you never knew where your next food was coming from.

There was a platter of thick-sliced smoked ham, with a dish of fried eggs and a huge bowl of hash browns. There was also trout and mushrooms, with gallons of coffee sub, loaves of bread and salted butter and maple syrup.

When, finally, Dean pushed away his plate and failed to suppress a great belch, it was time for them to be going.

Coburn had been curious about where they planned to go and what they planned to do when they got there. But Ryan stonewalled all questions.

"We catch you and we hang you. Hang you all," the sec boss repeated.

"Sure I know that. You coming after us on horseback?"

"No. No reason to. Deep snow like this, reckon we'll be up with you before nightfall. Mebbe sooner than that."

The two men shook hands one last time.

IT WAS WAY BELOW FREEZING, the snow packed tight and hard, and a bright sun poured down from a sky of chem-storm purplish-pink.

Ryan led the way, with Krysty at his heels. Then came Dean with Mildred, Michael and Doc. J.B. brought up the rear.

The old man found the going difficult, laboring with the exertion, his breath hanging in the still air. "Altitude and I were never the best of friends," he panted. "I don't suppose that it might be possible to snatch a short rest, would it?"

Ryan checked his chron. "Been going almost exactly two hours," he said. "Posse'll be on our tracks now. We've done around six miles. Mebbe seven. If we keep moving, then we should reach the trail up to the redoubt by late afternoon. Sorry, Doc. Have to step it out best we can."

J.B. had discussed the idea of his waiting behind and sniping at their pursuers. "Slow them down some," he suggested.

"Be a good number of them," Ryan countered. "And Coburn's bright. Knows the land around. Could circle and cut you off. No, fast and hard's the only ace on the line we got."

"CLOSING WITH US." Krysty shaded her green eyes, peering back to the valley behind them.

They'd climbed up a winding snake-back trail to a narrow ridge and had stopped to take five.

But the tiny antlike figures of Coburn and his sec men were visibly nearer.

"Barely an hour," Ryan said. "Let's go. Least we can see where we're heading now. Be at the foot of the last climb in about two hours."

"I'M MOST dreadfully sorry, my dear fellow, but I have reached the end of what is often called the tether. I do not believe I am able to set another foot forward."

Doc was slumped on the floor, head between his knees, fighting for breath. His face was as pale as polished ivory, and a thread of spittle trickled from the corner of his lips.

Mildred had knelt to examine him, checking his pulse. She looked up at Ryan, concern in her eyes. "Not so good," she said.

They were more than a third of the way up the steep track toward the concealed entrance to the redoubt. Ryan had been pleased at their rate of progress, seeing that Coburn and his men were gaining on them very slowly.

Now they were probably within three-quarters of an hour of them, but the slope was almost sheer and they, too, would have to slow down.

Light was failing as they climbed in the lee of

the mountain. The packed snow was becoming ever more icy and treacherous.

"Doc, we can reach the entrance in about thirty minutes or so. Take it in short spells. Go fifty steps, then rest awhile. That way you can do it." Ryan reached out a hand to the old man.

Who took it. "Do my best. Lean on my cane. When the going gets impossible then the impossible get...get something or other."

ONE OF THEIR PURSUERS attempted a shot with an M-16, but the bullet was wide and short. Ryan considered trying for Coburn with the Steyr, but he held off the idea.

They were now within a hundred feet of the ledge. Dean had slipped once in his eagerness, but Michael had grabbed him by the arm and kept him safe.

Ryan looked around at his group. "Nearly there. You okay, Doc?"

"I am a degree or two less than adequate, but I believe I shall accomplish the zenith, the perhelion of... Or should that be aphelion? I always become a trifle confused with—"

"Doc," Ryan interrupted.

"Yes?"

"More climb and less talk."

THEY MADE IT just as dusk was closing in across the Colorado mountains.

Doc threw up, shoulders shaking, head trembling. "By the Three Kennedys!" He wheezed a shuddering breath. "Once inside, can we snatch a rest?"

"Sure. Jump in the morning. We've all earned a break. How far are they, J.B.?"

The Armorer was peeking over the rim of the plateau. A shot rang out, but he didn't even move. "Still way off effective range. At least three parts of an hour, Ryan. They've slowed more than us. Goin' to be full dark before they get here. And they'll never break in the sec doors without the number code. Impossible for anyone."

"GLAD WE DON'T HAVE to go anywhere near that big earth shift," Dean said, grinning nervously at his father. "Home of the bleached wrigglies."

Doc patted the boy on the top of his curly black hair. "Beware the lair of the white worm, my lad. Beware the teeth that gnaw and bite."

Ryan smiled back, his hand on the control panel. "Yeah. Take an awful lot to get me around that part of the redoubt again." He pressed three, then five and finally two.

"Open sesame," Mildred intoned.

The companions were filled with tense energy,

weeks were safely behind them
just ahead.

"What?" J.B. asked.

Ryan pressed the numbers again.

And again.

Nothing happened. The vast sec steel entrance remained immovably locked against them.

"Fireblast!"

Take
2 explosive books
plus a
mystery bonus
FREE

Mail to: Gold Eagle Reader Service
3010 Walden Ave.
P.O. Box 1394
Buffalo, NY 14240-1394

YEAH! Rush me 2 FREE Gold Eagle novels and my FREE mystery bonus.
Then send me 4 brand-new novels every other month as they come off
the presses. Bill me at the low price of just $16.80* for each shipment.
There is NO extra charge for postage and handling! There is no minimum
number of books I must buy. I can always cancel at any time simply by returning a shipment at your cost or by returning any shipping statement marked
"cancel." Even if I never buy another book from Gold Eagle, the 2 free books
and mystery bonus are mine to keep forever.

164 AEN CH7R

Name	(PLEASE PRINT)
Address	Apt. No.
City	State	Zip

Signature (if under 18, parent or guardian must sign)

* Terms and prices subject to change without notice. Sales tax applicable in
N.Y. This offer is limited to one order per household and not valid to
present subscribers. Offer not available in Canada.

GE2-98

Follow Remo and Chiun on more of their extraordinary adventures....